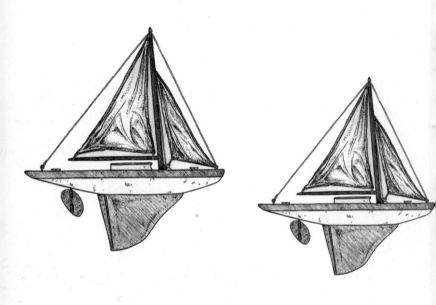

An

EXTRAORDINARY

THEORY

of

OBJECTS

An

EXTRAORDINARY
THEORY

of

OBJECTS

o   o   o

A MEMOIR OF AN OUTSIDER IN PARIS

o   o   o

STEPHANIE LACAVA

With Illustrations by Matthew Nelson

HARPER

www.harpercollins.com

I have changed the names of some individuals and modified iden-
tifying features, including physical descriptions and occupations,
of other individuals in order to preserve their anonymity. In some
cases, composite characters have been created in order to further
preserve privacy and to maintain narrative flow.

HarperCollins books may be purchased for educational, business, or sales promotional use. For information, please e-mail the
Special Markets Department at SPsales@harpercollins.com.

Illustrations by Matthew Nelson

FIRST EDITION

Designed by Leah Carlson-Stanisic

Library of Congress Cataloging-in-Publication Data has been
applied for.

ISBN 978-0-06-196389-6

12 13 14 15 16   OV/RRD   10 9 8 7 6 5 4 3 2 1

To those who unwittingly taught me about wonder in the world, to not be afraid of the dark, and to talk to strangers.

To Bryan, who taught me how to find them.

Are changed, changed utterly:
A terrible beauty is born.

—W. B. YEATS

*But men should not be too curious in analyzing
and condemning any means which nature
devises to save them from themselves, whether
it be coins, old books, curiosities, butterflies,
or fossils.*

—MARK RUTHERFORD

An

EXTRAORDINARY

THEORY

of

OBJECTS

Introduction

I was always strange. Born with red hair to parents without it, I always thought I was a changeling—swapped at birth because some perfect couple knew they didn't want me, even before I could talk, before I could tell them they were right. As a baby, I was disturbed by the quietest sounds and shadows on the wall. When I was older, a lover would call me out for odd behavior. "It must be a pretty planet you come from." He'd laugh at how I hated loud music and chaotic places. "You've fooled everyone," he'd say when I begged to go somewhere private. "People think you're normal." Years later, a friend would tell me a story about the time a well-known writer asked how exactly to "hang out." An anecdote meant to mock my lack of social ease. I imagined there was nowhere on earth where I could feel settled.

o o o

My outsider status was confirmed when my father took a job in France and my family moved from New York to a cold, empty house in Le Vésinet. I was twelve years old. From then on, I would never be quite American and, by virtue of my birthplace, never truly French either. The unsuccessful transplant began one April in the early nineties. Everything that represented my past life and its predictable ways—my geode collection, a jar of shells from summers in Cape Cod, a box of empty cicada skins—had been packed and placed on a containership slowly crossing the Atlantic. I arrived with my mother and brother, Zach, two months ahead of our belongings, and for that time I slept on a cot and wore the same shirt and pants every day to school. I started to obsess over my missing objects as evidence of what I'd lost. All I wanted was something to look forward to, someone beyond my family to want me, and to capture and tame the forces that caused this change. So, I started a new collection.

Back then, I trusted everyone and everything, but in particular the things I could hold. Most children latch on to the security of objects, but I went further. I was obsessed with cabinets of curiosities, historical efforts to catalog and control nature's oddities. A favorite example was the encyclopedic collection of rare flora and fauna that the Holy Roman Emperor Rudolf II kept at Prague Castle in the seventeenth century. I had a twin passion for ancient mythologies. These stories were another way to make sense of the nonsensical. Alone and unaccepted by other girls, I also loved biographies or fiction about alluring and iconoclastic women who would come to feel like real-life companions. Reading was a Pascalian diversion; stories and facts were a distraction from spiraling thoughts. I had always hated loudness. It was loud enough inside my head.

This mania extended to animals, people, and places—a city, even strangers in the street. I had a game where I liked to imagine what sort of pajamas each passerby might wear. This came from a belief that the more I know about the inner lives of others, the more I might understand the world. Collecting information and talismans is a way of exercising magical control. You can hold a lucky charm and know everything about nature's creatures yet still be terribly lonely.

o   o   o

When I fell apart at thirteen in France, I didn't lose my unfounded trust in others and the naïveté that ruled my youth, but I did misplace innate excitement, hope, and a will to live. A loss of control in my surroundings contributed to an active, throbbing depression. Spending those first full days in Le Vésinet alone—cut off—led to interactions with only objects and stories, which came to form the map of my breakdown and survival. What saved me, in the end, was my fear of change transforming into raw wonder and wanderlust. Intense sensitivity can be debilitating, or it can increase the upside of chance and the power of whimsy—a need for storytelling, strangers, and odd encounters. My strength with the written word is the ability to make unlikely subjects somehow connect, a capacity that has never been my strong suit in life. I had never been patient enough to believe that looking back my sadness would all make sense. But it does now.

It is with all apologies to my mother and father that I tell this story, as our family has always been intensely private. Growing up, I had plenty of love from my parents and brother, but I wanted another kind of comfort. In our family, value was placed in working hard, being compassionate and open-minded, not in frivolities or material indulgences. For me, though, there was safety and security in lovely little objects that appeared in the form of tiny souvenir-like tokens found over the years. My father found this same magic thinking in antiques or museums. Always gone for work, he became a treasure hunter in my imagination, a mustachioed pirate sailing across the world; it was my mother who kept order. As parents, they did nothing wrong, except encourage a lack of cynicism and foster creative spirit. It never occurred to me to be careful of life as a small child, to cultivate a second system of defense aside from my unusual instincts, to be guarded, aware, and patient with people in showing themselves. When I was little, it was sweet to lack social inhibitions and common sense. It became a handicap soon thereafter.

As an evolving adult, I am left with what happens when you grow up filtering the world through a very particular point of view—images are enlarged and cataloged with a classification dreamed up from my crazy years of a short life. I traffic the world using my idiosyncratic senses, so it follows that I'd document my life through a narrative illuminated with objects and their respective stories. The truth is, I can't relay everything exactly as it happened, because I'm not even quite sure of what happened. I remember that time in France in cinematic flashbacks filled with scenery and elaborate sets but rarely any actors. When I first wrote the narrative strand of this story, the objects came to me within the memories. I did not plan for so many connections or for the themes that emerged in this collection. When I was young, I didn't know all of this history. If anything, the only original link was my taste for these objects, an odd sensibility honed from the very events and scenes in which they first appeared. Then a web started to slowly show itself, a net to soften the fall from my memories. I researched the objects to own them by giving each new meaning and exorcising the old. During this process, I found peace in the lack of randomness of what I thought were childish fixations.

The ties between entries came in three distinct ways, and certain people reappeared throughout the stories. There was Lee Miller finding solace in photography and serving as a muse to Man Ray. Meanwhile in Le Vésinet, the Marchesa Casati fashioned her own immortality, captivating and entertaining artists and writers, Ray among them. When I think of a shell, I remember a scene in Françoise Sagan's *Bonjour Tristesse*, which is in itself a story of a precocious teenager learning about the world and sexuality, which also calls to mind Jean Seberg (see Seberg footnote on page 137). Both battled premature success and the pitfalls of fame and projected public adoration. Furthermore Miller was from a small town outside New York City, which happens to be the same place I was born—all three of us found identity in France. I am in no way comparable to these women, but what we share is a tendency toward eccentric or creative takes on our own circumstance.

There was also Oscar Wilde, with a taste for lilies of the valley; scarab rings on both hands; his residency and death at L'Hôtel; and even his novel, *The Picture of Dorian Gray*, as an example of the haunted pictures and phantasmagoria popular in the nineteenth century. The Victorian age and its archaeological obsession and revival of Greek and Egyptian styles lent another common facet to the list, as did the increase in the study of natural sciences like zoology. There was also the nineteenth-century thinkers' obsession with optics and the occult. It was during this time that famed French taxidermist Deyrolle established his business, due to the popularity of entomology and animal curiosities.

I had people, an era, and then finally a theme—an extraordinary theory of objects. As humans we crave beauty and we attempt to hold on to this experience through physical evidence. For religion it may be a relic, for the curious, a found talisman. For me, it is my story of conquering another world, a place where in order to survive I needed to seek out wonder. It was this unchecked romanticism that evolved into an adult skill to challenge sadness with words and a belief that what you experience isn't what is simply handed to you. Maturity means allowing for change and ephemeral feelings. It took a study of objects for me to see that if we are patient and gentle in observing ourselves and others, we will find connection. That has been the greatest comfort of all.

o   o   o

I never imagined I would live as I do today; I don't think I even believed I'd make it past twenty. Romantic love and calm were the great, elusive intangibles. I can now sit still for the length of a film, though my mind wanders. Love has come in unlikely forms and continues to surprise me. And the objects are still there, but only as mementos of more profound observations.

o   o   o

Here is my story, but told in a strange way.

o   o   o

Consider the source.

New York

Fall 1992

When I was eleven, I decided to buy land in Brazil. It cost around fifty dollars, brokered through a mail-order conservation society. Two weeks after sending in payment, a sheet of paper arrived entitling me to an acre of rain forest. I thought that if I ever needed to run away, the plot would be there, undeveloped, with hundreds—thousands—of *poison arrow tree frogs** surfing

---

* Nature rarely showcases useless, impractical beauty, but it can be tricky with its intentions. Poison arrow tree frogs' colorful skins are the furthest adaptation from camouflage, rather aposematic markings signaling to predators that the paper clip–size creatures can kill. Over one hundred varieties of poison arrow tree frogs exist, and they continue to evolve into new species and colors called morphs. There are frogs with red backs and periwinkle-speckled legs, black and yellow or mint green mirrored-spotted bodies, even one that is entirely electric blue. Surprisingly, if kept in captivity these little beasts can lose their poisonous defense over time. It is thought that this happens when they no longer feed on a particular insect found in their natural habitat. In the wild, among the greatest dangers for the

in wait for me. In the meantime, I had created the Amazon in my bedroom. Little figurines of the neon creatures were arranged throughout my bookshelves, while my walls were painted jungle green bordered with my best attempt at illustrated macaw parrots. My mother had let me decorate however I liked. I spent hours setting up my plastic frogs, finding the perfect spot for my favorite blue-and-yellow-speckled one. My love for him led me to lie on my bed, with its banana leaf sheets, and daydream of where I'd find his family and other crazy beasts. I didn't know then that I would soon have to leave this safe, make-believe rain forest.

---

frog is the very element necessary for its survival at birth: water. Torrential downpours can cause the tiny specimens to be swept away with the rain.

South American Indians would use the toxins from these rainbow skins to coat blowpipe arrows, hence the amphibian's name. For the most poisonous frogs, arrowheads needed only to be pressed against the skin. Other frogs were speared and heated over a fire to extract the venom. Legend says that certain indigenous tribes would rub a variety of the poison on the skins of young parrots to make their feathers fill out in different colors, a process called tapirage. It is believed that European traders may have adopted this practice to tint the common canary and then sell it as an exotic bird.

o   o   o

I learned of the upcoming change in the parking lot of a strip mall just outside of Boston. We were in Massachusetts for Thanksgiving with my grandmother, at the grocery store for some milk and life-changing news.

"You've always wanted to go to Paris," my father said, staring at me from the driver's seat of the car. I knew his face as a composition of two brown dots and a neat half-moon of facial hair that moved whenever he spoke. Sometimes I would watch his *mustache** instead of looking

---

* Giambattista della Porta was known as the professor of secrets for his keen obsession with finding a formula for nature's marvels. In 1558, the Italian scholar took teachings of the ancient world, matched them with his own experiments, and published *Magia Naturalis* (*Natural Magic*), using empirical studies to explain extraordinary phantasm, from the occult to alchemy. The famed mustachioed Salvador Dalí became a fan of this accounting of wonders. In the book *Dali's Mustache*, a collaboration between photographer Philippe Halsman and the surrealist, Dalí cites della Porta's belief that mustaches—and eyebrows—act as antennae to transmit inspiration. He and Halsman spent months working together with strobe lights, aquariums, even a hunk of Swiss cheese, to create a book about the many shapes that Dalí's mustache might take. There were figure eights and bows, and the question of whether this facial hair was

at his eyes. He was always calm, measured, and unflappable, like a spy from the movies. Based on his demeanor, elusive work, and routine travels, I believed he was a real-life secret government agent. My father was rarely in the States for longer than three weeks, and I spent so many hours imagining him that he'd become something of a myth.

"We're moving to France," he said.

I laughed. He did not.

"Seriously, Stephie."

"Why?" I asked.

"My job. I have an assignment overseas."

"Can't you just travel like you already do? Make a lot of conference calls? You could use that computer mail Prodigy-thing you just installed?" Before we left for the holiday, my father had shown me some strange device called a modem, which he

---

eclipsing Dalí's fame as a painter. One page pokes fun at the decline from beard to mustache in Communists from Marx and Engels to Lenin and Stalin. This list of history's greatest mustachioed men goes on to include Edgar Allan Poe, Mark Twain, Gandhi, Albert Einstein, and Friedrich Nietzsche. At the close of the book, Halsman says, "The great lesson of Dali's mustaches is that we all must patiently or impatiently grow within us something that makes us different, unique and irreplaceable."

plugged into the computer to send written notes over phone lines.

He shook his head. There was nothing for me to read. He rarely showed physical evidence of emotion. I was the opposite. The tears came immediately.

"I—I'm not sure I want to leave my friends."

"You never stop talking about travel; and you tell us how you don't really get along with the girls here, except for Ashley and Claire."

I bit my bottom lip and shook my head. He was correct. "Yes, but this is different."

"Not so much. It's a great opportunity for you and your brother."

"How?"

"Stephie, you will get to live in another country and understand it in a real way."

"What does that even mean?"

"Trust me, it's different from taking a trip. You know little of what else is out there." The mustache did not move. I had no choice but to trust him.

He didn't know that for all that opportunity there would be just as much pain.

New York

Spring 1993

I clutched my backpack to my chest as we cleared
security at the airport. My long, unruly red hair
kept getting tangled in the straps. My mother was
occupied watching my brother as he tried to run
ahead to the gate. She didn't ask why I chose to
hold the bag so closely. The man at security didn't
either. He waved me past. No one looked inside
to see what I was carrying with me. Buried beneath two stuffed frogs, an *ancient Egyptian
sarcophagus**—shaped metal pencil case, and a

---

* Until 1920, mummy powder, made from the ground-up
remains of looted tombs, was a cure-all offered in pharma-
cies. This serves as evidence that such wrapped-up bodies
continued to enchant long after their creation as they lay
hidden within anthropoid-shaped coffins. Ancient Egyptians sometimes decorated these caskets with feather patterns believed by some to represent a human-headed bird,
the Ba, the rendering for the unique soul. Ba comes into
existence only once a person dies and may revisit the body.
For this reason, a bejeweled soul amulet is often placed on
the mummy as a spirit guide. The term *sarcophagus* is de-
rived from the Greek words *sarx* and *phagein*, which mean

Discman was a large, *curved whale's tooth.*[*]

"flesh eater." Oddly, it was believed by the ancient Greeks that a body in limestone would quickly deteriorate.

Whenever someone died, embalmers would remove the organs and use natron powder from the Nile to treat the body. The corpse would then be left for forty days with someone standing guard until it was taken to the wabet, or house of purification, to be re-treated, stuffed, and sewn up. For the burial, servants carrying the possessions of the passed would follow a priest dressed as Anubis, the jackal-headed god of the underworld, into the tomb.

[*] Sea ivory is New England's very own contraband, made of the bone, teeth, or horn of a walrus, narwhal, or whale. Particularly illicit were scrimshaw artifacts from the nineteenth century, when the whaling trade was booming and the men at sea were restless. As fishermen grew impatient and lonely, they took to carving the by-products of their haul, creating art known as scrimshaw. Chapter fifty-seven of Herman Melville's *Moby-Dick* is titled "Of Whales in Paint; in Teeth; in Wood; in Sheet-Iron; in Stone; in Mountains; in Stars," calling out this pastime. Once a suitable surface was found, it was polished with sharkskin and prepped for etching. A knife or sail needles—any sharp object would do—was used to cut into the piece. Patterns were everything from fashion plates found in *Harper's Weekly* to whaling vessels and mermaids. Illustrations could be transferred using the pinprick method of dotting the lines through the actual page and then connecting the markings. Indian ink, spit, lampblack, and tobacco were all rubbed into the grooves to illuminate the picture. Perhaps

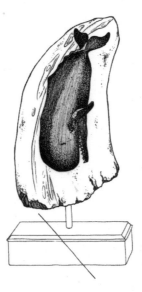

the most coveted work was a busk, a gift for a love waiting patiently at home, made of a slab of bone that would be
used as a stay in corsets. As recounted in my letter exchange
with scrimshaw historian Donald E. Ridley, the art form
was short-lived, though, with the discovery of petroleum.
With kerosene readily available, whale oil was no longer
needed for lamps, nor was a remedy for the monotony of
being alone at sea.

My father had given the ivory piece to me some time ago, knowing I would keep it safe in my collection. I was told I had started stockpiling pretty things when I was three, beginning with a foil-covered egg I didn't realize was chocolate until a friend took a bite. The whale tooth was a souvenir from one of my father's Nantucket holidays as a child. I loved it. Not only did it belong to him, to his mustache and gentle heart, but the tooth also symbolized fantasy. To me, it could have been the horn of a narwhal, or part of a Minotaur, though neither was as exotic as my father. I could read about these creatures, whereas there was no guidebook for my parents. Before my father left to go ahead of my mother, brother, and me to France, we had all sat together at the kitchen table to discuss our strange future.

"Where are we going to live?" I had asked.

"We found a house." The mustache did not move.

"A house? Don't people live in apartments in Paris?"

"We're going to be just outside the city, in a town called Le Vésinet." It suddenly made sense why my father and my mother had gone overseas a month ago and left us to stay at my friend Claire's house. "Zach will have a backyard to play in, and you will love the park there, Les Ibis. It is filled with swans and there is a special pink palace, the Palais Rose." I couldn't listen. I was angry with him for not asking us, for not even telling us, until the arrangements were all settled.

"Why didn't you tell me?"

"It didn't make sense to share the news until it was all set. You will go to a small international school in Neuilly-sur-Seine."

I felt as though I was being briefed like one of his colleagues, which made me feel grown-up.

"We will leave the third week in April. You will start school the day after your birthday. You will fly with your mother and brother, as I will already be in France, working and making sure everything is ready. The movers will come and pack what we won't need right away to be shipped in a container at sea and arrive in a few months. Put aside what you'll need sooner. We are keeping our house here, so you can leave certain things behind."

I didn't answer. Anything I would have said would be cut with sarcasm, which my father would not appreciate.

Again came the tears.

o   o   o

The whale's tooth lay hidden in my backpack as we boarded the plane.

"Stephie, are you ready?" my mother asked. She tried to take my hand. I pulled away. The move could not have been an easy decision for her; she would play single parent much of the time in a foreign place. Yet I blamed her, because it was easy—she was emotional, but not fragile. I was both.

"I'm fine."

I held the tooth beneath a blanket the entire flight.

Le Vésinet

Spring 1993

Upon arrival in France, I unpacked my little sack on the wooden floor of my new, empty bedroom. There was a large arched window on the left wall covered in rusty white-metal shutters that I couldn't figure out how to open. I stayed in the dark, exhausted to the point where I could barely sit up. One, two, three, there they were: my whale tooth, my poison arrow frog, and the sarcophagus pencil case. I lined the objects up around me on the floor where there was a little light coming through the slits of the shutters, so each one sat on a sunbeam. I spoke to the frog, "Welcome to France, I know it's not quite the rain forest." He didn't say anything in return.

o   o   o

I woke up later that night with my head nestled on my backpack. It was completely dark and very cold. A blanket was at my feet. My mother must have come in while I was sleeping. I had no idea what time it was or if anyone else was awake.

There was a little light in the hall outside the door. I stood up and lifted the blanket, wrapping it around my shoulders. It was quiet; everyone was sleeping. I walked softly through the hall and down the stairs. There was another light coming from outside. I went across the kitchen and un-latched the back doors. A half-moon was in the sky over a broken-down little house that must have belonged to the gardener. I decided to have a look, trampling a few yellow tulips before find-ing myself at a rotting gray door. It opened easily, letting some little creature out with a gust of stale air. Inside, the floor was covered in shards of terra-cotta pots and remains of a stained glass window. I kicked something that made a sharp clang as it hit the wall. It was a *skeleton key.**

---

* Consider the power of the early locksmith: his skill was synonymous with security, and knowledge of his craft was hard to come by, as talented locksmiths didn't want to share their secrets. Henry II of France's locksmith cre-ated a famed master, or skeleton key. An agitated king, frustrated with the many keys required for the doors of his castle, including that of his mistress's chamber, prompted the innovation. Later, Henry III would have a similar key created for his mistress, Diane de Poitiers. There is evidence, however, that skeleton keys date back further to when ancient Romans used a system of warded locks. The

key was a romantic notion in the Middle Ages, for it would open not only doors but also coffers filled with treasure and castles where women were held captive. In 1568, the young William Douglas rescued Mary, Queen of Scots, from Lochleven. As the two rowed to safety, he dropped the key that freed her into the water. It was eventually recovered and landed in the hands of Sir Walter Scott.

With keys, came locks, and also lock pickers, whose ingenuity matched that of the locksmith's—tapers would be lit and a keyhole smoked to get the wax impression of the inner mechanics, or a mirror would be angled upward to examine inside the hole. The idea of a master key can even be seen within mythology. Greeks believed the queen of the night and witchcraft, Hecate, held the key to the complete spirit world and magic.

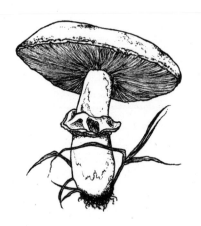

Le Vésinet

Fall 1993

I bent down to pluck a *mushroom** from the wet

----

* The classic storybook mushroom with its red cap and white spots is the drug of choice among Siberian-dwelling reindeer. One bite and they may find themselves in a drunken stupor, the same for a fly that sips the toadstool's juices. This variety can be found all over the world. Farther south, there are other sorts of intoxicating, even more enchanting, species, like those uncovered by R. Gordon Wasson, the Montana-raised financier known for his knowledge of cultural attitudes toward mushrooms. It was this interest that led Wasson to Mexico in 1953 on a quest to learn about the hallucinogenic plants eaten by the natives. There he met a Mazatec *curandera*, or healer, María Sabina, who introduced him to the world of psilocybin mushrooms. Shamans were known to eat these little beasts and be overcome with language. In 1955, Wasson and his friend Allan Richardson, a New York–based fashion photographer, became the first Westerners to take part in the nocturnal mushroom ceremony known as *la velada* in Huautla de Jiménez. When *Life* magazine published Wasson's findings in the article "Seeking the Magic Mushroom," unforeseen consequences followed, including an eager clan of celebri-

ground. Clusters of them had sprung up along the path to the park. I sank deep into the mud, my new sneakers covered in thick brown paste. My mother had finally allowed me to buy a pair of skateboarding shoes like the other kids at school. Kneeling, I tried to keep my feet in the air as I pulled at the plant with its red cap and cream-colored spots. I braced my legs against a tree, lifting my thin slip dress to let my knees touch the earth. It was difficult to see. The sun wouldn't rise for another two hours.

I liked to walk alone in the dark. The first time I had tried a late-evening stroll was two days after our arrival in France, the night of the skeleton key. Sneaking out at night became my escape from days

---

ties, from John Lennon to Mick Jagger, wishing to be part of the experience. Wasson hadn't intended to sell out Sabina, though she was quickly ostracized for sharing the secrets of the natives' society. She never, however, regretted meeting Wasson. Rather, she'd foreseen their encounter. In later years Wasson, who detested the word *hallucinogens*, preferred to use the word *entheogens* instead, which means "god within." He considered himself above all a scholar and bibliophile obsessed with words found in old books. This preference was probably a reaction to a pop culture that was spiraling out of control, much like the misinformed public perception of mushrooms.

filled with books and silence, a boredom verging on insanity, locked inside with my little belongings and endless ruminations. My brother too had become uncharacteristically quiet and withdrawn since the move, shutting himself in his room, leaving only for a croissant from the kitchen before returning to his toy cars. He had always shown signs of being odd, evidence that I wasn't a changeling after all, but his behavior, like mine, grew stranger by the day. He, my mother, and I moved through the house, airy versions of our old selves, coasting over the cold marble floors. My mother's Oriental rugs wouldn't arrive for another month, the same for her toile de Jouy curtains, and the same for her husband. He'd been traveling for much of the year. The entire house was hollow and icy, even though it was only early September. It was warmer outside.

I had taken a pale tan *cardigan** with me when I

---

* How did a half-pullover, half-button-down knit become synonymous with both grandfather dressing and grungy insouciance? The sweater was first invented in the nineteenth century, owing to the vanity of James T. Brudenell, the seventh Earl of Cardigan. He was tired of having to disturb his hairstyle when changing his look and so decided to create a collarless jacket, which unbuttoned from the front. Fast-forward to actor Steve McQueen, who was among the

famous men to adopt this style. Most iconic, however, was the trend in the nineties when kids hit vintage stores to seek out old, ratty cardigans for sale, to emulate the pilling sage one Kurt Cobain wore onstage for his unplugged performance in New York in 1993.

left the house in case the wind stirred up as the sun started to rise over the streets. The left shoulder of the sweater slipped off, exposing the thin strap of my dress, as I yanked at the mushroom. The root gave way, and I fell backward. The slip flew up, and my bare bottom hit the ground. My back and legs, like my sneakers, were now covered in dirt. I stood, shook the dress down, and pulled the cardigan on, all with my left hand, as my right held tightly to the mushroom. The freshly picked plant wouldn't last forever, but long enough to sit on a shelf and lend its charm to my new collection.

There were more patches of mushrooms huddled together at the corner of the street leading to the park. The mottled markings on my skin matched the patterns on their hats. I knew the park Les Ibis wasn't far from rue Ampère, where we lived, but I wasn't sure exactly how to get there, and I couldn't ask anyone. The few women I walked by looked at me with disdain, because of my sneakers. They were dressed in long skirts or tiny fitted suits with heels. I didn't care, feeling rather invisible anyway. I was the French cartoon character Fantômette. By following a young woman pushing an old-fashioned stroller, I found the entrance. We took two rights and a left, past a roundabout and the green painted gate. Two swans stalked nearby with beady eyes and orange beaks. One ducked its head into the neck of the other. This one then flicked her wings and spread her orange web toes as she waddled back into the water to float among branches and fallen leaves. Her friend followed, and they both coasted toward the Palais Rose across the pond. The mansion looked like a film set, with its pink-and-white pillar marble façade and massive black-and-gold gate. I read its history off of the plaque on the ground. In 1900, Arthur Schweitzer had commissioned the mansion to be built after the Grand Trianon at Versailles. It was then sold to Ratanji Jamsetji Tata for three pearls and an emerald. The next owner was Comte Robert de Montesquiou, Proust's "Professor of Beauty." There, in Le Vésinet, Montesquiou entertained the likes of Sarah Bernhardt and Auguste Rodin. In 1922, the *Marchesa Luisa Casati**

---

* In 1881, the Marchesa Luisa Casati was born in Milan. The shy, plain heiress, fascinated by dramatic figures like Sarah Bernhardt, grew up to establish herself as an auburn-haired, green-eyed, live-snake-wearing eccentric who walked her big cats through the streets of Venice and arrived at the Ritz with her boas and cheetahs in tow. She drove a blue Rolls-Royce often accompanied by a towering manservant. Among her houses was the Palais Rose, where Man Ray, Jean Cocteau, and Cecil Beaton were all occa-

came to live at the Palais Rose with her library of books on the occult, pavilion of portraits, mechanical panther, stuffed boa constrictor, Blue Rolls-Royce, and wax effigies.

That morning, as my sneakers grew soggy in the manicured grounds, I stood in front of the grand house, trying to imagine its old owner, the insane and beautiful Marchesa Casati. I thought I saw someone in the window with almond eyes, holding a candle, though the image was only one of many daydreams. They happened often, because I was so unbalanced: on the best days, I experienced a realism deficiency with an excess of whimsy. Some people's bodies need to make extra blood cells or insulin for survival; mine manufactured fantasy. This marble palace at the end of my park was comfort against the creeping tediousness of my days and odd new faithless impulses. I had to try to sort through what exactly I was doing in this foreign place. The swans honked, and I stepped backward.

---

sional guests. Countless artists painted Casati, and she was muse to many as well as the lover of Gabriele d'Annunzio, who called her Kore, another name for Persephone. Despite creating a legacy destined for immortality, Casati died in 1957, destitute, skinny, and scavenging for objects to adorn her frail body.

Without quotidian American distractions, I became aware of my thoughts as I never had before. My growing insecurity wasn't rooted in anything specific that happened, but rather what didn't happen. It was on walks like this that I began to notice how my head dealt with the world. I wasn't wired for contentment. All these fears, all these thoughts, they wouldn't stop, unless I buried them with stories and random information. Numbers suddenly became important to me. I liked to do everything in even counts. Some superstitious reasoning told me that odd meant something bad would soon happen.

Not once that morning had I considered the feelings of my mother back at the house, perhaps terrified, looking for me in an empty bedroom as the sun rose. I knew it was insensitive, but I couldn't bring myself to go home. Instead I walked around Les Ibis exactly four times and then toward town.

There were two shopping areas in Le Vésinet. The larger one was just beyond the silver stag roundabout with streets of gourmet shops, a general store, and an ice-skating rink near the site of the outdoor market. I walked toward the older, smaller center with its boulangerie, épicerie, North African traiteur, and papeterie. It had been over three hours since I'd left the house and I was feeling unusually hungry. I had a ten-franc bill rolled up in my shoe.

The man who ran the épicerie was a small, tan Algerian who spoke in patient unintelligible words. I liked him from my first visit to his shop, with my mother, to find some milk. He had offered me an electric-colored candy from the plastic bins he kept stacked by the cash register. I had chosen a red ribbon covered in little sour crystals. He recognized me immediately. I was thankful he was open so early.

"Qu'est ce que tu veux?" he asked, looking at me with gentle eyes.

I lifted my shoulders knowing very little French yet.

"Des bonbons?" He pointed to the stacked clear containers.

I nodded, not caring that this would be my breakfast. Those sorts of societal conventions had never meant much to me: mealtimes, talking in turn. He passed his hand over the bins of green frogs with crème bellies, sunny-side eggs with yellow centers, and rainbow sour strips. I shook my head. He lifted his finger.

From beneath the counter he pulled out a lovely little oval box printed with two lovers amid tiny purple flowers. I nodded. He pried it open, and inside were sugar-dusted *violet candies.*

I'd never eaten anything flower flavored before, but I picked one up and placed it on my tongue.

---

* The violet is one of the few flowers that flourishes in the winter. It can be found in dark, cold months, its resilient buds pale purple with a dust of frost. In the thirteenth century, apothecaries sold crystallized violets—roses and lilies, as well—steeped in hot water and sugar as a cure for all ailments. It was in the nineteenth century that the violet trade flourished north of Toulouse, France, where there grew a renowned variety with twice the amount of petals in comparison to the standard bloom. During this time, violet-flavored sugar crystals and candies were popular delicacies sold in decorative tins and used on pastries. Further back in time, the Romans would soak violet petals in casks of wine to create the celebratory drink, Violatum. Violet was always a favorite scent among royalty, including Napoléon, who was given the name Corporal Violet when he promised to return from exile in Elba with the tiny flowers, which he did in 1815. It was then that he left a bouquet on the grave of Empress Joséphine before being exiled again to Saint Helena. At the turn of the twentieth century, it was rumored that the empress of Russia Alexandra Feodorovna used an eau de toilette made exclusively from violets that were picked between the evening hours of five and seven o'clock in Grasse. The allure of the violet lies not only in its perfume but also in its beauty without ostentation.

It was wet, natural, and sweet, like I imagined the earth would have tasted had I taken a handful from the lawn in front of the Palais Rose and shoveled it into my mouth.

I left the little man with a small bag of the violet candies. He had refused my ten francs and insisted on giving me the sweets. I'd never been in a shop alone with its owner, nor one where we couldn't communicate, but we shared something of a bond. After all, he wasn't from France either. I paused for a moment in front of his green-and-yellow-striped awning with a white-spotted red mushroom in one hand and a bag of purple candies in the other. The sun had come up, lighting this part of Le Vésinet to resemble a scenic throwback to seventies small-town America. A Deux Chevaux crackled by a roundabout planted with primary-colored tulips and lilies of the valley, which would arrive from beneath the ground in the spring. I wasn't sure I knew how to get back to rue Ampère, to my house, and to my mother and brother inside. But I started home, eyes fixed on the street.

Then, I saw it: a violent blue spark in the sidewalk, which quickly paled to discrete white, like a shy phantom. It sparked again, this time, illuminating purple and pink. I bent over, holding the mushroom in one hand while letting the candy fall

to the puddle-covered ground. My knees, caked
with dirt, began to drip mud. I pulled my cardigan
up over my shoulders as I picked up the glittering
object. With my free hand I lifted the thing as if
it were the tail of a snake covered in creamy blue
and lavender spots. I was holding an antique *opal
necklace,** somehow lost and forgotten. It may

---

* The opal is not one color; rather, it's every color. Even
covered in dirt, an opal may shine red or blue, sparkling
in its dusty raw state. Pliny the Elder spoke of the opal's
magic in *Historia Naturalis* ("Some opali carry such a play
within them that they equal the deepest and richest colors
of painters"), where he also mentions that sugar acid may
be used to make a virgin stone black, as jet and fiery red
opals were more dramatic than their pure white counter-
parts. Like the tapirage method used to dye the feathers of
common canaries, this chemical trick created the illusion of
more desirable specimens.

Just as mummy powder was thought to be a cure-all,
ground opal was also thought to be a remedy for endless
maladies. The stone was also believed to bring good luck,
impart prophetic powers, cure depression, and even help
blond hair retain its shine or detect poison by paling in its
presence. Napoléon gave Empress Joséphine a 700-carat
black opal, while Queen Victoria was known to favor the
stone as a present on special occasions. Sarah Bernhardt in-
creased the renown of the gem, her birthstone, as she commissioned art deco jewelers like René Lalique and Georges
Fouquet to create unique pieces such as the snake-shaped

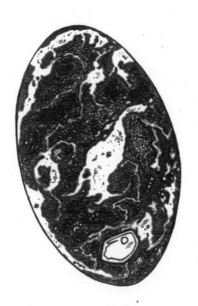

have been exhaustion, or simply my anemic common sense, but it didn't strike me as that strange
a discovery or that it belonged to someone else. I
picked up the candies and continued walking back
to the house with my mushroom, violets, and fiery
jewelry.

o   o   o

A few days later my father was finally back. The
last time he'd been in France was prior to the first
shipment of furniture and before setting off to

---

gold bracelet with attached ring, which she wore for her
role as Cleopatra at the world premiere in 1890.

Yet there has always existed a darker, more foreboding
side to the opal. Many feared its mystic powers, a phobia
said to have started with a scene from Sir Walter Scott's
Anne of Geierstein, in which a princess dissolves into ash
when the opal in her hair is splashed with water. It was a fear
somewhat grounded in reality, since, owing to their porous
nature, opals may self-destruct with too much moisture or
heat. In the late nineteenth century, Alfonso XII of Spain
received an opal ring as a present from his spurned lover,
the Comtesse de Castiglione, which he in turn gave to his
wife, who soon died. It was then given to his grandmother,
Queen Christina, and passed down through generations
who succumbed to similar fates. In the end, the only solu-
tion was to hang the ring from a chain that dangled around
the neck of the Virgin of Almudena of Madrid.

North Africa, or somewhere like that. He was at my bedroom door.

"Come in, Dad." As I sat up he ran over to me and gave me a hug.

"I missed you."

"Then why did you go for so long?" I asked. He said nothing and the mustache didn't move.

"What's this I hear about you bringing fungus inside?" My mother had been begging me to throw away the plant I had put on the shelf as part of my collection.

"It's my mushroom."

"And you need it here on your windowsill, why?"

"Look at how beautiful it is!"

"That is one nice mushroom," he said.

"Please, Dad, don't be like Mom, she's annoying enough."

"How about I make a deal with you?"

"What?"

"You lose the mushroom, and I take you somewhere special today filled with things just like it—better things, things you can't even imagine."

"I don't believe you."

"Have I ever lied to you?" It was true; every crazy thing he'd ever said had come true.

"Fine, take my mushroom." I sighed as I

watched him walk over to the windowsill, crawling with little black bugs.

"You still have the tooth I gave you! The one from Nantucket."

"Yes, I like it."

"I loved that tooth when I was little. I took it with me everywhere. What's that key for?" he asked.

"I don't know."

"We will have to find out. For now, get dressed, we are going on a little trip."

o o o

It took us an hour and a half with traffic to drive from Le Vésinet to our destination in Paris. My father planned to park in a garage, which meant our car had to be inspected first by police. Everyone was on high alert because of the recent bombings by Algerian insurgents. My father showed the men his papers, and they seemed satisfied after a quick sweep of the backseat and trunk. When they were done, we drove down one level and found an empty spot. Neither of us said a word as we got out of the car and locked the doors. I quietly followed my father into the elevator to the ground floor. When we stepped onto the street he motioned me to the left, and we walked two blocks before reaching the

entrance to the Muséum national d'Histoire na-
turelle, the museum of natural history.

"We're here," my father said as we took our
place at the end of the ticket line behind a tall
teenage boy and his girlfriend. I suddenly felt
self-conscious, having barely brushed my hair. I
was wearing a blue-and-white long-sleeve sailor
stripe sweater underneath a yellow T-shirt, and
loose, faded black leggings with my skateboarding
sneakers. My hair was matted and tumbling down
my shoulders in gnarled red strands. I watched as
the boy took the girl's hand after they paid and led
her into the museum.

"Stephie?" my father said.

"Yeah?"

"Where are you? Let's go." He put his hand on
my shoulder and steered me to the main hall.

There, at the heart of the museum, was a
taxidermy parade: a timeline of stuffed animals
from prehistoric reptiles to present day. An enormous scaled lizard led creatures like a fat woolly
mammoth, Indian elephant, Bengal tiger, and
big-horned ram. I loved their beady eyes and
frozen bodies and that unlike their dynamic for-
mer selves, they could go nowhere. They were
enduring objects rather than beasts. "You see
that?" my father said, pointing ahead. "That's

a real *dodo bird.** They're extinct now. You can't

---

* How did a fat, ugly bird descended from the common pigeon become one of the most mysterious and romantic creatures of the natural world? Perhaps this fascination is largely because of all the extraordinary circumstances surrounding its life and discovery. It was around the turn of the seventeenth century that the birds were identified, only to become extinct sixty years later because of humans settling the dodos' habitat. The dodos lived on the south coast of the island Mauritius in a swampy land known as Mare aux Songes, nearby the Indian Ocean. Without natural predators—that is, until men arrived—the birds flocked inland, where food was plentiful. They had no need to fly, so their large wings soon became useless, purely ornamental. Modern imagery of the dodo bird comes from an obscure painting by the Dutchman Roelant Savery, who died in an insane asylum in 1639 in Utrecht. Most mythology surrounding the bird began with the drawing of John Tenniel and Lewis Carroll's *Alice's Adventures in Wonderland.*

As chronicled in Errol Fuller's *Dodo: From Extinction to Icon*, in 1865 schoolmaster George Clark found there were dodo bird bones beneath the marshy ground of a nearby sugar plantation, which he ended up selling to anatomist Richard Owen, much to the displeasure of his rival, Alfred Newton. It is believed that until 1755 the Ashmolean Museum had the last remaining specimen of the long-extinct dodo. After a meeting of trustees, it was decided that the piece had rotted beyond repair, but fortunately they salvaged the head and a single foot. In 2007, scientists found the most complete dodo skeletons to date in a cave in Mauritius. Undoubtedly the dodo's short life and scientific

find one anywhere." But there one was, with its squat, feathered body and curved beak.

---

speculation about the extinct bird's actual appearance contributed to its allure as one of nature's most controversial creatures. That and they have become an early example of humanity's ability to sabotage the natural world.

"How many are there in the world?" I asked, immediately enchanted.

"I think this is the only one left."

"No?"

"Yes, unless you count those that survive in stories."

o   o   o

We'd been in France for over six months, well, more like four, considering we'd spent the summer back in New York. Instead of growing familiar, my surroundings became filled with more curious customs, places, and people, but I no longer felt the excitement of initial discovery. Les Ibis, the Palais Rose, Paris even, I went to all of them each week, and while they still managed to mesmerize a little, they weren't enough to keep me from falling into a kind of numbness. Somehow cynicism had crept over my fantastical thinking. I was mostly alone that year. I rode the bus to school and listened to my Discman while the girl in the back row threw gum wrappers at my head. The girls at school didn't like me very much. They had never given me a chance, decided immediately that I didn't belong, which was funny, as they didn't either—at least not in France. They made me feel as if I had done something wrong, and they spoke badly about me to each other. Through my own odd rationalization, I decided excommunicating me meant they belonged to something, simply because I did not. They didn't like that I had a growing friendship with the boys, either, although the one I wanted most was taken. I had met all twenty of the other people in my grade, and none of them seemed quite right for me. If I did the math, one over twenty was the fractional equivalent in the world of negative-something-crazy over all the people out there, which meant there wasn't much chance at a real friend. Despite being so young, that's how I thought, in fatal absolutes and always in numbers.

Come the new academic year, the old class would be replaced with another set of students who had just moved overseas. Only a few remained year after year—and still the same insensitivity.

o   o   o

My family celebrated Halloween that October, as Americans tend to do. My brother and I hung white ghosts in the trees of the backyard and carved pumpkins. Our neighbor proceeded to complain to the town about the pagans living next door. As pagans, we also celebrated Thanksgiving together, while none of Europe did at all.

Much of the American population would take off to Euro Disney for the expatriate version of the holiday feast. My brother, mother, and I followed them. My father was away. There, we ran around and rode the rides before congregating for a faux turkey dinner at the Buffalo Bill's theme restaurant. The only problem was that I couldn't relax and enjoy the insanity of the whole scene: five hundred misplaced Americans in a cartoon fantasyland. I became obsessed with checking every gift shop, looking for the Alice in Wonderland section and maybe a stuffed dodo bird.

Le Vésinet

Spring 1995

I hadn't left my bedroom in two days. My mother had tried to get me to come out for meals, but I'd refused. It was my plea to be recognized as prisoner-in-residence. I didn't eat all that much anymore. My face was permanently gaunt and red, a shade lighter than my hair, from hours of crying, and my body was pale and weak from the ongoing hunger strike. It didn't matter that my mother, my father, and my brother all loved me. I only felt dramatic rejection of everything. As a family we'd taken trips I should have been thankful for; to the rocky beaches in Marbella, the tiny town of Bruges, and then the last winter, skiing in Courchevel. Yet, on every holiday, I spent my time looking around for something else, waiting for someone to notice me, trying to engage with strangers, hoping to feel some kind of excitement. Inspired by Cécile in *Françoise Sagan*'s* *Bonjour*

* Writer Françoise Sagan was born in 1935 in Cajarc, France, where she would be buried sixty-nine years later.

Tristesse, I sought an understanding of grown-up affairs—and attention from grown-up men. Cécile had admitted that she was "more gifted in kissing a young man in the warm sunshine than in taking a degree." It worried me that I was the opposite; I'd never kissed a boy, but school had never been a problem. I was dedicated to my studies; they distracted me from the other part of my mind. When Cécile mentioned she was trying to write an essay about Pascal, I immediately knew all about him. Adult attention, though, was only another daydream, as no one cared for a skinny little elf girl. I didn't want to swim or ski, I only wanted to know what it would be like to sit and laugh among friends or with a lover. The part of my mind that was supposed to rationalize a pragmatic approach to problems was led by an automatic calibration of negativity. It was a chemical sadness, a slowly growing depression.

She reached unprecedented literary success at the age of nineteen with the publication of the seminal *Bonjour Tristesse*, for which she won the Prix des Critiques. Great celebrity followed, elevating Sagan to mythic status. A fan of fast cars, she nearly died in an accident when driving her Aston Martin in 1957. Over time, her fame began to fade, not unlike the young bright light that was Jean Seberg, the star of the 1958 film version of *Bonjour Tristesse*.

There was a knock and then shuffling footsteps. Someone had pushed something under the door. I stood up from my bed. I'd been wearing the same pale nude slip dress for the past three days. After listening to make sure no one was in the hall, I slid the door open and found a tiny bouquet of *lilies of the valley** with a note on the floor. I had for-

---

* With white bells sheathed in green leaves, the lily of the valley is lovely, but deadly. The flower is so poisonous that those who handle its blooms are cautioned to wash their hands after. Despite this warning, the plant still signifies purity and the coming of happiness. Oscar Wilde and couturier Christian Dior both favored the flower. The blossom was also the namesake for Lily Bart in Edith Wharton's *House of Mirth*, perhaps a symbol for a desire for poisonous perfection and exhibitionism. The title of Honoré de Balzac's 1835 novel of society and romance translates in English to *The Lily of the Valley*. *Muguet*, as lilies of the valley are known in France, are sold by the roadside for loved ones on May 1, based on the legend that the flower loved a nightingale who would only return to her when she bloomed in the late spring. According to other lore, lilies of the valley sprang from the blood of Saint Leonard of Noblac when, having grown disenchanted with royal life, he battled with a dragon in the woodland he wished to inhabit. Further back in history, Eve is believed to have cried tears that turned into tiny bells as they fell when she was exiled from the Garden of Eden, just as the Virgin Mary's tears turned into the same flower at Jesus's crucifixion.

gotten it was May 1, the day when the French cel-
ebrate hope and spring and give the tiny flowers
to loved ones. I opened the piece of my mother's
cream-colored stationery. "I grew these for you,
Love, Mom." It was true. She had planted them
when we arrived. So much time had gone by since
then, nearly two years, and now they were here
and I wasn't any longer.

I knew it was incredibly thoughtful. The little
blossoms looked perfect on my vanity's glass shelf
next to the whale's tooth and tiny frog figurine.
My collection had grown too large for the windowsill. I sat on the carved wooden stool in front
of the round mirror and combed my tangled hair.
I was newly aware of a tingling in my stomach
and thighs that made me crazy to find someone,
to think about sexual affairs, a fantasy love life. I
wanted to be a player in the adult world. I imagined that a special man would give me the hope
and confidence I lacked on my own. Yet instead
of leaving my room to find him, or even make a
friend, I shut myself inside. I preferred to sit on
my bed Indian style and reread my worn copy of
D'Aulaires' *Book of Greek Myths*. I liked to learn
the details of each deity and try to pair him or her
with someone I knew. It was a way of organizing
everyone, fitting them into a system. The Greek

gods were like people, but more beautiful and could do nothing terribly wrong.

I imagined I would like to be Iris. She seemed so lovely and carefree, wearing a dress of iridescent water droplets, making her way along the rainbow. And if I were a greater goddess, perhaps I would be Aphrodite emerging from a shell, my naked body covered in *pearls.**

---

* Found within the mouths of oysters, these tiny iridescent balls have come to signify rare beauty. When Aphrodite rose from the sea within an enormous shell, she cried tears of pearls. Pliny the Elder tells the story of Cleopatra's wit and cheek, which involved wearing earrings created from the largest pearls ever discovered. She summoned Mark Antony for the most expensive dinner of all time in which she dissolved one of the pearls into her glass and proceeded to drink its contents, leaving him dumbstruck. Cleopatra often wore pearls wrapped twice around her neck, or in her hair, or a shorter piece to accompany a dress embroidered with the tiny white orbs.

The gems were rare in Egyptian jewelry, and it is said that Julius Caesar tried to create sumptuary laws that restricted the wearing of pearls to only Rome. Later in history, the second wife of Henry VIII, Anne Boleyn, also known for her intelligence, wore a signature pearl necklace hung with a gold *B* pendant and three teardrops. Sara Murphy, owner of Villa America and the inspiration for Nicole Diver in F. Scott Fitzgerald's *Tender Is the Night*, was often seen wearing pearls down her back.

My match was more Persephone, though, kidnapped into the underworld. Even her name sounded like mine.

At the top of Olympus was a girl in my grade named Charlotte. She had been at our school the longest, since kindergarten. Brought up in Switzerland, she spoke perfect French and was very pretty, with a small nose and ample chest. Her father was a powerful banker, her mother somehow connected to royalty. They lived in a two-floor town house, and her bedroom was still decorated with Ludwig Bemelmans's characters from *Madeline*. She always had crumpets from Marks & Spencer, the English store with shops throughout Paris. Her sister had already graduated and gone on to Lawrenceville in New Jersey for high school. When her sister visited she always wore punk-grunge clothing, like shirts from the brand Fuct or Stussy, or one of those orange-lined green bomber jackets from an army-navy store. I believed Charlotte led the other girls against me. She'd been there forever. It was easy to trust her word.

Then there was Natalie. Perhaps less interesting than Charlotte, though more beautiful, she was an army brat from California who had moved around her whole life. She was known for French-kissing under tables in the cafeteria and twirling her hair. She was the real Aphrodite. I admired her sexy, brazen ways. She sometimes talked back to Charlotte and always to our teachers.

Sarah's father was the CEO of some company that made things no one understood. She had moved to France from Connecticut, not far from the town where I had lived back in the States. Her thin blond hair was always pulled back in one of those silver clips you'd find at an American drugstore in the nineties. Sarah was Athena, smart and sturdy.

As for the boys, there were three who were particularly intriguing, and sometimes kept company with the above. Jake had moved to France from Tokyo and his father ran an American bank. He loved Nirvana, Red Hot Chili Peppers, Quentin Tarantino, and Pamela Anderson. Navy blue sweat suits were his uniform of choice. He and I had similar spirits, and it may have been this bond that made me a little uncomfortable with him. Instead of embracing his quirkiness, I was sometimes repelled by it, because it mirrored so much of my own. Jake was American and best friends with Raees, who was half South African, half American. The two of them were inseparable, always making movies together with Jake's camcorder. I had fallen in a teenage love-obsession with Raees. Whereas Jake was just like me, Raees wasn't at all. He seemed stoic and confident and didn't really know that I existed, unlike Jake, who, in his own weird way, seemed to care about me. Raees's mother was a purported spy, newly married to a Swedish prince. Maybe she knew my father. Here were Apollo and Aries.

Michael, I knew only for a little while, as he decamped with his family to Rome soon after my arrival at school. He played Zeus, at least from what I had heard, for the duration of his rule.

Other classmates included Aashif, whose father was the ambassador from Kuwait, and Akiyo from Japan with his rocket-scientist mother. He was close with Seiya, who was also Japanese, and best friends with Palat, a Thai prince. They always seemed to have the latest gadgets and technology. They were the Three (Eurasian) Fates.

In the older crowd, there was a brooding boy named Tim, who was Hades. Then there was Sophie, who was Helen of Troy, beautiful and cool. She was dating a boy who was a skater—rough and rather grown-up and the brother of her best friend.

Among the younger children were Titans like Melanie, the daughter of the founder of the most fashion-forward store in Paris, and Henrik, the son of a famous tennis player and a model. He would grow up to be a professional basketball player, celebrated in his own right.

After some consideration, I decided that if I could choose, I would want to be Artemis, a waif-like virgin hunting goddess, rather than Iris. The mythology game worked well as a method of classification and exposition on character. That is, until everything went upside down. Problems started in our teenage lives because there wasn't the security of a Poseidon character to summon *rain*,* wipe out tragedy, and pacify uprisings and betrayals. We realized authority governed only in theory and as a construct of its own creation. We became aware

---

* An earth ravaged by rain is a universal myth, though details may differ. Before Noah's ark there was the myth of Deucalion, which is similar to the Old Testament story of the great flood. Outraged by the insolence of his people, Zeus decided to flood his kingdom and rid the earth of humankind in its then state of disgrace. Deucalion's father, the Titan Prometheus, learned of Zeus's plan and helped save his son and his son's wife, Pyrrha. Deucalion built an enormous boat-box similar to a chest that allowed him and Pyrrha to arrive safely to Mount Parnassos. By throwing the bones (rocks) of their mother Earth (Gaia) over their shoulders, they were told they could repopulate the earth, Pyrrha creating a race of women and Deucalion a race of men. There are no animals or ark in Deucalion's story, but rain still stands as a symbol for rebirth and one of the only forces humans may be able to predict but can in no way control.

that teachers and parents couldn't control what we thought they could when one of our classmates died of cancer and someone's father committed suicide. Around the same time, one of our teachers explained that when Kurt Cobain sang "Rape Me," he meant it metaphorically, which became useful in social studies as a way to understand Rudyard Kipling's feelings about imperialism. I learned to play basketball in an empty pool at the American Church. Instead of crossing guards, men with machine guns sometimes stood watch at the school gate.

At least once a month, there was a bomb threat and we had to evacuate a few times. The news often reported the Algerians clashing with the French. Every time there was a Métro bombing, I worried that my father had been among the casualties. It mattered little that he was usually not in Paris at the time; I always assumed the worst.

o   o   o

It was the sound of rain starting to fall slowly outside my window that made me finally leave my room come nighttime. I stood up, unhinged, and pushed open the rusted shutters to look into the garden. It was the perfect weather for a walk. I padded quietly down the marble stairs, through the kitchen, to the back door, which opened quietly. I was barefoot and the stones on the landing felt cold beneath me. I walked slowly with my head lifted to the sky, catching the raindrops in my hair. The shower was still soft enough that I could sit in the garden without shelter. There was a circular cement pedestal littered with birdseed offerings nearby the shed. I pulled myself up onto it. Again, I lifted my head to the sky. Something started to crawl over my foot. I looked down, and there was a *beetle*,* its shell burnt red with black markings. I

---

* Oscar Wilde wore a green scarab ring on his left hand signifying happiness and one on his right hand to symbolize sadness. When asked why he didn't remove the latter, he said the absence of happiness was necessary to understand the very nature of contentment. Long before Wilde, scarab amulets were popular as protective talismans. In ancient Egypt, the dung beetle was the model for the scarab as a symbol of rebirth. These beetles would roll balls of dung out of which came their next generation, just as the sun, or Ra, rolled through the sky with each new day. It was Aristotle who named the class of creatures coleoptera, from the Greek words *koleos* for "sheath" and *pteron* for "wing," as the wings of the beetle are encased in two hard shells. During the Victorian era the allure of the scarab was revived with an interest in the romance and mystery of Egyptian tombs and the occult. Jewelers would use actual iridescent beetle shells and wings to create pieces. Charles Darwin was a devoted beetle collector. The natural history museum in Paris houses the greatest collection of speci-

tried to pick it up, but it opened its wings and flew away. Then I noticed all the other beetles. They were everywhere—shiny chartreuse shells, big black monsters, ladybirds, and tiny brown ones. I watched them tour the slab I had sat down on before escaping into the backyard at large. One went straight for the lilies of the valley. The rain began to fall harder around me. I had once read that beetles were the most diverse and populous species. I was comforted knowing there was nowhere I could go where I wouldn't be able to find some kind of beetle to keep me company.

---

mens, many now extinct; however, still one in every three insects remains a beetle.

Paris

Fall 1995

"Stay there," Jake said. He was waving his beer bottle at me with his left hand. In his right hand was a camcorder. I was sitting in the grass of a park just outside of Paris trying my unsuccessful best to be enchanting. Jake and I were sort of "going out," but I translated that into trying to play muse to him and Raees. I liked him very much, but not in the same way I lusted after Raees. There was no way I could have said no when he asked me out (it didn't mean on a date, but rather to officially be his instant-girlfriend). He and Raees were my friends, and I couldn't risk losing them. That and I desperately wanted to be like *Lee Miller** was to

---

* Lee Miller was born in April 1907 in Poughkeepsie, New York. From a young age, she was entranced by the camera's ability to distance her from reality, perhaps because of her own childhood trauma of being raped and contracting a venereal disease. A great beauty, Miller captivated men, including Condé Nast, who serendipitously saved her from an oncoming car in the street one day, which led to

Man Ray—the video cameras and seventh-grade screenplay version. Miller had been troubled kind of like me and still managed to find someone, an artist, to love. She was beautiful, stylish, and independent, everything I was not. I tried my best too: a pale nude *slip** with a striped, ratty lime green cardigan I'd found at the vintage store Kiliwatch,

---

her start as a model for magazines like *Vogue*. She went on to become Man Ray's lover, muse, and protégée, and then a talented photographer and war reporter in her own right. At the end of her life she is said to have grown depressed, perhaps owing to not only the time she spent photographing concentration camps but also the roving eye of her husband, Roland Penrose.

* Perhaps the most indelible images of the nineties slip dress are those of Kate Moss in a loose, nude negligee either in a magazine editorial or out with friends. Or maybe it's a singular moment, Carolyn Bessette Kennedy in the simple white wedding dress her friend Narciso Rodriguez created for her wedding to John F. Kennedy Jr. The style itself was created anew in the nineties with the designs of Calvin Klein and Helmut Lang, who in the late eighties presented a seminal collection of simple silhouettes, rejecting the overwrought styles of the time. John Galliano's take on the look, bias cut silk, often with tiny Victorian silk buttons, was another version of this iconic slip dress. During this time vintage became cool all over again, and thousands of girls channeled Moss in thrift store finds or versions from the mall.

in Paris. There was nothing to fill the bodice of the dress, save for my efforts at charm. The outfit was chosen for my screen test as Lady Macbeth in Jake and Raees's next film collaboration, *Macbeth: The Dice Decides*. They had just shown their short of *Rosencrantz and Guildenstern Are Dead* in the school auditorium. I knew the audition would involve some drinking, smoking, and filming, so I'd tried to dress accordingly, my only sources of style inspiration: my mother and my magazines. I knew all about the current models, like my favorite, Karen Elson, with her bright red hair and pale skin. She was sometimes referred to as Le Freak, which worked for me. Then there were Guinevere van Seenus, Shalom Harlow, and Trish Goff. I loved all of them, especially Amber Valletta in the Prada ads, as she floated away on a boat in Southeast Asia. I didn't distinguish between advertisements and editorial. My floor was covered in glossy, torn-out pictures, like those of Harlow wearing neon stripes in Gucci ads alongside a redheaded model with her hand suggestively on her lap.

"There's a hole in the elbow of your sweater," Jake said as he changed the CD from Smashing Pumpkins' *Mellon Collie and the Infinite Sadness*

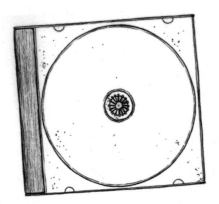

to *Nirvana*'s* "Smells Like Teen Spirit" on *Nevermind*. He and Raees often talked about the music videos they'd seen on MTV, one of the few English-language channels. Music seemed to be the main way American culture seeped into France. I always felt I was experiencing a little of the life I would have had back in the States when we listened to certain bands. Perhaps this wishful nostalgia is the reason I fell in love with fashion too. That and I was painfully skinny and

---

* In 1991, Nirvana released *Nevermind* in a square plastic case with the standard pull-out pamphlet, except this album had a controversial photo that would come to represent grunge for some. Under the art direction of Robert Fisher, Nirvana's team wanted an image akin to water birth, which Cobain had witnessed on a television program. Critics have said he chose this image as a means to hold on to innocence, but others believed it was a statement on selling out, whether it be as a band or leaving behind the yuppies of the eighties. The irony of the whole grunge movement and Nirvana's rise to fame was in Cobain's rejection of being the voice of a fringe generation. It's said no one expected Nirvana to explode out of Seattle as the face of grunge, a movement made during days of darkness and boredom. It was the grunge band Mother Love Bone that was poised for stardom until its lead singer died of an overdose in 1990. And then, somehow being alienated and isolated became mainstream.

awkward-looking, like a tall elf, and so were the models of the time.

I ignored Jake's comment about the hole. He had transitioned from sweatpants to broken-in corduroys, which he wore with flat skater shoes and four layers of T-shirts in different washed-out colors with a long-sleeve thermal underneath. Raees had on a similar look, but with torn jeans and a blazer he told us he'd found in his father's closet. I thought he was beautiful. It wasn't his blond hair or height, but a certain stillness within him, a calmness I craved for myself. I had noticed he wasn't quite like the other boys but more laid-back and witty. He was the brain behind the Abott Charles Dingie Administration, a faux group of jester pundits, which had grown into a full-blown political ruse that now included campaign posters hanging in the halls at school. No teacher took the flyers down, complacently encouraging the whole scheme. I liked Jake and his quirky sensibility and creativity, but he was like me— introspective and creative. This was the problem.

"Steph, you want a beer?" When we were among friends we always spoke in English, even though most of us were fluent in French. I could understand everything I read, though my writing, especially verb conjugation, could stand some improvement.

"Sure." When he turned away to film the trees

behind us, I spilled the can's contents onto the ground.

"So, guys, what do you think of this setting for the witches scene?"

"It's cool," Raees said. "Though, we would have to film at night."

"I love parks when it's dark. Remember that night in the Bois de Boulogne?" Jake asked. I wasn't sure if I should mention my night walks, maybe they were weird.

I figured their new project would be a little like the upcoming version of *Romeo and Juliet* with Claire Danes and Leonardo DiCaprio I'd seen previews for, rather than the Zeffirelli version we'd watched in class, the teachers stopping and restarting the film to explain the play. Their argument was that it was akin to going to the Globe Theatre and seeing the Royal Shakespeare Company. But how does one translate Lady Macbeth into the nineties?

"Steph, do you have a costume to wear?" Jake asked.

"I have this dress that's a Scottish plaid, which I could wear with red Doc Martens?"

"Scottish, like Scotland. Good. Red, like blood on Lady Macbeth's hands. Excellent."

"So, what now?" Raees asked.

"What do you mean?"

"I'm satisfied with this spot, and we're out of beers, and we've listened to both albums in full."

"I guess we go back," Jake said, reaching for my leg. I inched away from him into the puddle of beer on the ground.

I saw Raees the next day at school, but Jake never turned up.

o   o   o

"Your father's in the basement," my mother said when I got home one afternoon from school. It was a month after Jake's weeklong disappearance. He'd returned to school as if nothing had happened. We all knew it had to be something serious by the way the teachers whispered and nodded. Of course, I was supposed to be his "girlfriend," but he didn't mention anything to me, so I thought better of asking him. Clearly we had a healthy, normal relationship. I was in love with his best friend and didn't know how to communicate with either of them.

I rounded the corner down the stairs to find my father. "Daddy?"

"Stephie!" he called to me.

"I am so happy you're back. Why do you go for so long?"

"Work," he said, bending down to pick up a stud that had fallen out of his hand.

"What are you doing?" I asked. He had a hammer in one hand and squat nails in the other. There were silk foulard scarves all over the floor where he'd dismantled the base of three antique *chairs*.[*]

My mother had warned him against buying the trio, but he'd believed he'd find the fourth one somehow, somewhere. He was busy reupholstering

---

[*] In antiquity, chairs were not commonplace; rather, they were seats of power. Stools were used as everyday furniture, whereas thrones were reserved for high society, like those found in Tutankhamen's tomb, and were carved of precious materials with animal legs. In ancient Egyptian reliefs, pharaohs are always depicted sitting upright to signify their status. Akhenaton, father of Tutankhamen and husband of Nefertiti, was portrayed, however, as reclining, perhaps in satire, as he was an early supporter of monotheism, which was contrary to the nation's longtime polytheistic devotion. In ancient Greece, the klismos chair was created with its curved back and tapered legs and was later adopted by French Directoire, English Regency, and American Empire styles and even by Ludwig Mies van der Rohe. Saint Peter's Chair, which is in Saint Peter's Basilica, is not merely a piece of furniture but is also a relic as famed as the Dagobert chair now in the Louvre's collection. Though the seat is missing, the bronze frame is believed to have been owned by Merovingian king Dagobert I in the Middle Ages, with the arms and back added by Charles the Bald in the twelfth century. It was then used by Napoléon I for the Légion d'honneur.

the seats with scarves he'd stolen from her drawer. I had no idea where he got this idea or if my mother had any idea it was happening. Nonetheless, her Hermès carousel scarf was being tacked onto the seat of a dark wooden frame. My father gestured for me to hold the corner of the fabric while he pinned it down. "Do you want to go with me to the *brocante* to look for the other chair?"

"You actually think you'll find it?"

"Why not? It could happen."

"You're serious?"

He nodded. "I had an idea earlier, why don't you decorate the library here however you like? You can do some research and make the room whatever you imagine. It will be the perfect place to put our Minotaur and Hydra." One of our activities when my father was in town was to create papier-mâché animals. We used assorted materials—tape, balloons—anything to construct the bodies of the beasts I'd read about in my mythology books. We then covered these creatures in wet sheets of plaster of paris, which hardened to life as cardboard skins.

I liked this idea, especially as I'd just read about this eccentric decorator named *Madeleine Casta-*

ing.* Unlike many of the women who captivated me, she had been alive the year we moved to France. I wish I had known to ask my father to take me to see her. He would have loved that she would sell her own flea market finds based on the value she felt for them or the desire of the potential owner, regardless of the object's material worth. This is how my father conducted his treasure hunts.

"I need to tell Zach to get ready. He's coming too, no?" I asked.

---

* The inimitable decorator Madeleine Castaing was born at the end of the nineteenth century in Chartres, France. Known for her eccentric personality and style (late in life, she wore false eyelashes with a black wig tied at her chin as a makeshift facelift), she carried this unique sensibility over into her interiors. Castaing loved literature and channeled Balzac and Proust, which she claimed to have read twelve times, in her décor. There was never one style, rather a mix of the likes of Napoleon III, English Regency, and Russian neoclassical, even Gothic, with flea market finds, faux marble, or plastic flowers. She loved blue, hated beige, but adored black. Leopard spots or tiny, green foliage scattered on black carpet, banana leaves as window shades were among her signatures. Castaing claimed to be against perfection, finding beauty in the unlikely and unfinished treatment, such as fading painted stripes, or old objects. She died in 1992 at ninety-eight years old, leaving behind her world, which famously became a hard-to-catalog 2004 Sotheby's sale due to the mix of treasures.

"Sure," my father said. I ran up the blue stairs from the basement to look for my brother.

"Zach," I yelled.

"What?" he said, poking his head out of the bathroom where he was wearing swimming goggles while sailing miniature ships in the bidet. I laughed.

"Get ready."

"Should I bring my goggles?" he asked. I shouldn't have laughed, considering his odd behavior was further evidence of our shared genes.

"Your goggles?"

"To see the sea monsters."

"We're not going to Versailles." He'd always wanted to stick his head into the Grand Canal to see the fish there. "We're going to look for antiques."

"So boring." He rolled his eyes behind the blue plastic before running upstairs to put on some clothes. My mother came out of the kitchen carrying the wicker basket she sometimes used as a purse. "I packed a little picnic," she said.

My father walked the white marble stairs from his bedroom, looking like a vagabond with torn corduroy pants, a denim shirt, and an old Scottish sweater. Dressing down was one of his tactics for haggling with sellers. He took the picnic basket from my mother and gave her a kiss. She was wearing very long trousers that dragged on the floor over her heels and a silk blouse with a bow at the neck. Very seventies, very Yves Saint Laurent, very my grandmother. She was also wearing her mother's armful of gold bangles.

"Where's your brother?" my father asked.

"Coming!" Zach yelled as he slid down the stairs in his socks.

"That's dangerous. No socks on these floors," my mother said.

He rolled his eyes again. "Do we really have to go to this antique thing?"

"Yes, we are going as a family," my father said. We followed him out to the car.

ɔ ɔ ɔ

When we arrived at the market, my father stopped us at the entrance for a briefing. "Okay, so before we split up there are a couple of things we are in search of. One: I need an armoire for the dining room. I want something old, intricate, and carved with fish! No other sea creatures; no mermaids. Two: we need an animal of some kind, discounting the fish on the armoire. Finally, whoever finds the fourth chair missing from our set will be able to buy whatever they want within reason. Understood?"

We nodded. My mother smiled and squeezed my father's hand.

"Since this is a competition, we can't be together the entire time," I said to my father.

He thought for a moment. "This is true. Then we will rendezvous here in an hour. Agreed?" My brother was thrilled to be set loose on his own. He went off to the first stall on the left while my parents started at the far entrance. My mother was happy to have some time alone with my father.

I knew where I wanted to start the search. There was a young man who dealt in furniture, oddities, and old books down one of the rows. He'd once given me an antique copy of the complete works of Shakespeare, covered in pale cream fabric printed with green clovers. I knew he did it so my parents would buy something far more expensive, but the gesture had charmed me nonetheless. I found him sitting in a chair made of horns sorting through a box of old postcards. "Do you have any of Le Vésinet?" I asked in my best French.

He looked up and recognized me. "Ah, jolie mademoiselle, I do." He handed me two that looked like my favorite waterfall at Les Ibis and a house near the Palais Rose and rue Diderot. "Those are for you. You live there?" he asked.

"Yes." He looked to be in his thirties, handsome with stubble at his chin. His clothes looked expensive, but at the same time carefully eccentric. He wore a cardigan with leather arm patches, corduroy pants, and sneakers. I felt an odd sensation when he touched my arm to pass me the postcards.

"My parents live there too. This is really their stall. I just work here some days, because I find it interesting to meet people like you. But then I end up giving things away for free. I guess I am not much of a salesperson," he said, laughing. Again, I felt the strangeness in the pit of my stomach.

"How lovely, then what do you do?" I hoped he could understand my French.

"I am a writer and a philosophy student, I guess," he said, looking straight at me. I blushed. He must have known I was much younger. I was happy I'd worn some mascara that day. "What are you looking for today?" he continued.

"I'm decorating a room. I need to find some, er, taxidermy."

"That is quite a mission."

"Yes, well . . ."

"I have something hidden I can show you." He walked behind a pale green curtain and came back with an object in hand. It was a black window box

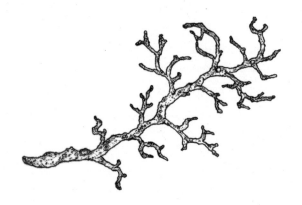

embedded with rubies flanked by two big *coral**
branches at each side. Inside was the tail of a beautiful fish attached to the body of a stuffed lamb's
head. It was meant to look like a sea-goat, which
reminded me of my papier-mâché projects.

"How much is it?" I asked.

"It's not for sale," he said. "I love it too much."
Once again, I turned red. "Although, I do have
this for you." He went back behind the silk sheet
and came out with a box covered in tiny iridescent green beetle shells. "Do you like it?"

"Very much."

---

* All coral—angel skin pink, black acabar, rare blue
akori, and Italian bianco or white—were once living as
polyp creatures fixed to other ocean fauna, cannonballs,
and even, as once documented, a human skull. The Mediterranean Sea and Italy are known for their coral, but it is
found in both the Atlantic and Pacific oceans as well. Even
so, it was an unlikely commodity traded between East and
West, as was documented as far back as the first century by
Pliny the Elder. Ancient Egyptians believed in the mystic
powers of the rosy exoskeleton and carved scarabs from
this precious material. The ancient Greeks believed it pro-
tected against poison and spells and was the petrified blood
of Medusa that dripped into the sea. From India to Tibet to
the Americas, coral is revered as an organic marvel turned
talisman, imbued with magical meaning, just like the oys-
ter's pearl.

"Do you promise not to tell anyone?"

I nodded.

"It's yours." Behind him, I noticed a large armoire, each door carved with fish.

"Thank you so much. That just caught my eye," I said, pointing to the piece of furniture. "Do you remember my parents? It's exactly what they are looking for."

"Well, I will hold it and you will bring them by?" he asked.

"Yes, please also hold the box until we return. Then you'll know I'll be back."

"This is our plan, little beauty. See you soon."

I walked to the next aisle, wondering if all he wanted was a sale. Only Jake had ever thought I was beautiful or appreciated my oddness. Why would a handsome older man? I nearly tripped over my brother, crouched above a chest on the ground.

"What are you looking at?" I bent over to find the box was filled with *glass eyeballs.**

---

* Ancient Egyptians would use clay eyes for both the dead and the living that lost their sight, using linen cloth to secure them within the sockets. Stone or glass suspended on a string eventually replaced these hand-painted balls. In 1579, Venetians created the first glass prosthesis to be

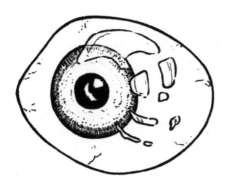

Zach was picking through them carefully, looking for something in particular.

"Aren't they amazing? I want to find ones that look like your eyes."

"My eyes?" I asked.

"Yes, pretty green ones," he said.

"For what?" I had a brilliant idea. "Dad said I could decorate the empty room downstairs. Why don't we get a ton of these and cover an entire wall with them?" I said to Zach.

"Cool!" he exclaimed. I went over to the lady in charge and asked the price.

"They're two hundred and fifty francs, about fifty dollars each." I reported back why we could never afford to do a wall.

---

worn within the eyelid. The French royal surgeon Ambroise Paré fashioned similar pieces from enameled gold, silver, porcelain, and, of course, glass. Elaborate hollow glass eyes began in Germany's Black Forest in 1832 when Ludwig Müller-Uri's young son lost his eye in an accident. Luckily, Müller-Uri happened to be a talented glassblower known for making realistic doll eyes by twisting strands of colored melted sand. Prior to this, peasant families were known for creating animal eyes used in taxidermy and similar pursuits. No matter how skilled the artisan, glass eyes can never see, but they alter what is seen before us.

"I thought they would be much less, all loose in this box," Zach said.

"Maybe we can find them at another dealer."

I followed him around the corner and up a row to stop in front of a set of bleachers covered in red velvet and filled with all sorts of taxidermy mixed with old stuffed plush animals. There were chickens, parrots, toucans, little dogs, a lynx, Mickey and Minnie Mouse dolls, and assorted insects set up in dioramas.

"What do you like the best?"

He pointed to an enormous snake in a plastic rectangular case that was bigger than he was.

"You know that pink marble house in the park?" I asked.

He nodded.

"The woman who used to live there kept her pet boa constrictor named Agamemnon stuffed in a display case when he died."

"Stop it, Stephie."

"No, really. It's true. She also had a life-size mechanical panther."

He rolled his eyes.

"Madame, do you know the time, please?" I asked the old lady who owned the snake.

"It's sixteen hours," she said.

"It's four o'clock, Zach, we have to get back to the meeting spot!" The woman smirked and turned away, pulling the cloche she was wearing down over her ears. We ran away to find our parents.

My mother and father were waiting for us, empty-handed except for the picnic basket.

"We found everything," I said. My brother nodded. "First, I need to take you to see the armoire." They followed me back to the stall.

"It's perfect," my father said, while the young man watched me. "How much is it?" The man quoted quite a large figure. My father bargained with him for a few minutes before they agreed on a price. "Stephie, good find." He paid and discussed arrangements with the man, all in English. It turned out he spoke rather perfect British English, and I wondered if maybe he wasn't French at all but an expat, just like me. "All done," my father said, and he and my mother started to follow my brother, who was excited to show them his discovery. I lingered behind. The man came over to me and whispered, "Thank you," as he handed over the beetle box. I didn't have the confidence to reply. I would never see him again.

Paris

Spring 1996

"He definitely wears a baby blue Onesie, the sort with feet," Jake remarked as he watched a man with round tortoiseshell glasses limp by us.

"Really? You think so?" I asked.

"Totally."

"What about her?" I pointed to a beautiful teenage girl with long, blond hair who was sitting across from us at the café.

"Black lace, for sure." I had expected that answer. "Maybe neon lace, the kind you wear sometimes." He was referring to an acid-colored camisole I wore with army green pants, a combination I had seen in one of my magazines. My surprise that he noticed my wardrobe mediated my disappointment at his comment on the other girl. Jake and I had "broken up" a few months ago, but nothing had really changed in our relationship. I still liked Raees, but Jake was the one with whom I spent time and flirted with confidence. I wondered what he thought I wore to sleep, but I never got up the nerve to ask him. We were never part of the *pajama** game, only strangers. Jake had taught the game to me: you had to guess what any passerby wore to sleep at night as a way of imagining his or her character. I had told him I played a similar game in which I watched people and guessed at where they might be going in the world. Both distractions were useful to manage the mystery of strangers. I found comfort in knowing that there was something unknown and interesting happen-

---

* Old guard couturier Paul Poiret was partly responsible for the start of pajamas leaving the bedroom for evenings out on the town. His popular satin harem pants began a trend continued by Edward Molyneux and Jeanne Lanvin, often with a pair of silk trousers worn beneath a tunic. The Allied governments encouraged daytime pajamas during the First World War. Silk, it was said, would keep you warm, and the easy silhouette allowed for work in the garden. The leisure class of the twenties and thirties, however, was already packing pajamas for vacation, along with their bikinis. Marlene Dietrich was known to wear them at the Lido in Venice, a style that eventually found its way stateside to winters in Palm Beach. In one of Zelda Fitzgerald's letters to her husband, F. Scott Fitzgerald, she wrote about how obsessed she was with her new pair of sleepwear: "They're the most adorably moon-shiny things on earth—I feel like a *Vogue* cover in 'em," she said. Later on, Kurt Cobain would embrace the trend in his own way when he wore green pajamas to his wedding.

ing in anyone else's life at any moment. Jake liked the game, because it helped him develop characters for his films. Raees just sat there, listening to us with a bemused look on his face. I imagined we were at a café like in *The Sun Also Rises*. I had always thought that the perfect woman was Lady Brett Ashley, appearing to be insouciant and happy. It would have been so lovely to be young in Paris if she and Zelda, Sagan and Seberg, all of them, were here with me, instead of Charlotte and her clique.

"Hey, you know who you look like?" Raj, one of our other classmates, piped in. He was sitting between Jake and Raees.

"No, who?" I asked.

"Angela from *My So-Called Life*.* It has to be

---

* The television show *My So-Called Life*, starring Claire Danes as fifteen-year-old Angela Chase, first aired at the end of the summer of 1994 at the 8 P.M. time slot on national network ABC. Later that year, *New York Times* journalist Matt Zoller Seitz wrote, "What the series' narration does best: it shows how teen-agers try to control their chaotic inner lives by naming things, defining them, generalizing about them." What everyone loved about the show was its authenticity—an unreliable, even unstable, narrator experiencing universal feelings. It was the outsider's answer to the vapid world of *Beverly Hills 90210*. In early

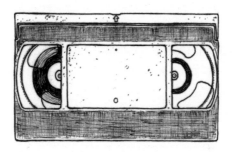

the red hair." I didn't know whom he was talking about, only that Claire Danes played the character on some television show I'd never seen.

"I haven't seen it."

"You haven't seen it?"

"No."

"Everyone's seen that show."

"It's not on television here."

"Don't you have friends in the States? They can send it to you." I didn't answer him. It was funny that although I didn't understand the references of Generation X, I knew all about the Lost Generation.

---

episodes, Chase dyes her hair a bright shade of red ("It's not red, it's 'Crimson Glow'"), leaves behind her childhood best friend, and falls for Jordan Catalano, played by Jared Leto ("I love how he's always leaning against stuff, he leans great"). The program was groundbreaking in its portrayal of the complicated teenage experience. In an episode, Chase comments on the yearbook: "If you made a book about what really happened, it would be a really upsetting book." Fans were disappointed when the series was canceled less than a year later. There were even ads taken out in the likes of the *Hollywood Reporter* to renew the series, which was eventually rebroadcast on MTV. The whole production was very nineties—ending in its prime so passionate viewers could still worship the show without inevitable disappointment.

"So are you stoked to go to Burgundy?" Raj asked Jake in reference to the weeklong trip our class would soon take to central France.

"I cannot wait. Raees is bringing his guitar, we're going to jam out." They both looked at me expectantly.

"Um, it should be cool. I'm excited to see the relics at the churches in Vézelay." They both laughed.

"You're one of a kind," Jake said, unexpectedly placing his hand in my lap. I pulled away.

"We'll have fun," he said. "Kind of like tomorrow."

"What's happening tomorrow?" I asked. The three of them just laughed.

o   o   o

The next day, we were sitting in English class, waiting for our beloved Mrs. Smith to start the lesson, but she refused to do so without Jake, Raees, and Raj, who had yet to arrive. All of a sudden someone screamed, and in ran three men, dressed in black with panty hose pulled over their heads. "Terrorists!" Charlotte screamed, and we all went under our desks as we'd been instructed to do during drills.

I kept my head down but could hear Mrs. Smith

laughing. These people are insane, I thought to myself, we're all about to die. I was shivering, trying to keep my eyes to the floor and my body as compact as possible. So far there had been no gunshots, and none of the masked men had spoken. I said a prayer of love for my family and tried to become even smaller, inching toward the door.

"Where do you think you're going?" someone asked.

I almost fainted but then realized the voice was familiar. Keeping my eyes downward, I tried to think of what to say and why I felt I knew the intruder.

Charlotte started laughing. Such disrespect would get us killed. They are all certifiable, I thought to myself. "Look at that idiot," Charlotte whispered. I could feel her eyes on me.

The same voice that had questioned me about my earlier movements spoke again. "You have all been taken hostage by the Abott Charles Dingie Administration."

All of a sudden I knew exactly who it was. Unfurling myself, I looked up at the front of the room. There were Raees, Jake, and Raj with panty hose pulled over their faces.

"It's all in good fun," someone said with a British accent.

o   o   o

I had trouble understanding the humor in the coup d'état incident. It would never have been allowed in an American school, but that wasn't what really bothered me. Crouched on the floor in the class-room, I'd only been able to think of Charlotte's insensitivity—and my father. I worried about him every day. It was selfish, but I needed him to help me figure out how to get out of my head, as my anxiety had become increasingly worse. He was so patient and calm. Why didn't I inherit those traits? I got only the crazy ones. He sensed I was nervous about the upcoming school trip, and the weekend before, he made sure he was available so that we could spend a special day in Paris together. We had decided to make two stops. First, we would go to the *catacombs** and then to the famed Parisian taxi-dermy shop, Deyrolle.

---

* Within catacombs, great religious men were laid to rest underground, before the furor over relics caused the pilfer-ing of these mass graves. The origin of the word *catacomb* is Greek for "cavity" or "below," which is apt to describe the massive, vast winding tunnels created for the bones of the dead. Eventually the term came to mean simply an un-derground tomb or crypt, once the caves were ravaged for relics. (See relics footnote on pages 111–13.)

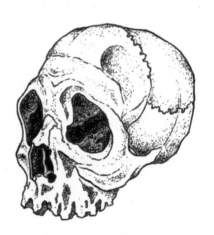

I had been begging him to take me to the cata-combs for a long time, but we'd never had the chance. Our last visit alone to the city had been to the museum of natural history over two years ago.

"Stephie?" my father said as he pulled the car out past the gate surrounding our house.

"Yes." I watched his mustache for any sign of emotion.

"I want to know what's going on with you."

"What does that even mean?"

"You know what I'm talking about."

"No, I don't."

"You haven't been yourself."

"I'm older now."

"Which means what exactly?"

"What did Mom tell you?"

"That she's concerned about you. That you lock yourself in your bedroom and take walks alone at night."

"Seems pretty normal to me."

He tried to hide a little smile and mumbled something inaudible.

"What?"

"I just want you to know, I'm here for you," he said more clearly.

"No, you're not."

"I know I'm away often, but that doesn't mean I don't love you and I can't help with whatever this is."

"You can't and it's kind of your fault."

"It is?"

"Yes."

"I have to travel for work. It is for our family, so you can go to school and we can do fun things together like today."

"I meant, it's your fault, because you made us move here."

"You think whatever's going on is France's fault?"

"You know what I mean."

"I don't."

"I was fine before."

"Steph, you always had this tendency."

"What tendency?"

"To be sensitive to your surroundings, to fixate on little things. It's chemical."

"I don't understand."

"You can't have these preconceived ideas in your mind about how life should be. Don't think so much. Do things you enjoy with people you love. Everything is always changing. What you can't control frustrates the hell out of you, no?" His mustache lifted as he asked the question. "But

I also love this about you. It makes you special. So, tell me what you're feeling."

"I can't, because I don't know."

"You have so much to be grateful for . . . ," my father said, and it was then that I first felt guilty for having my pain.

"Why do you want to go here so badly?" he asked as we pulled into the street leading to the catacombs. I kicked something on the car floor. It was my father's pair of binoculars.

He claimed he used them for bird-watching. When he had time to watch birds, I wasn't sure.

"Because I like seeing what's beneath the city and learning about death and rituals."

"Again, not so normal, Stephie."

"Yeah, well neither are you with your chairs and weird creatures."

"We make those guys together," he protested.

"Yeah, but they are your idea." I paused and thought about my accusation. "Actually, you're not like me at all. Maybe you're not even my real father."

This made him angry.

We didn't speak throughout the tour.

My father loved history and listened intently to the guide as we walked around the skeletons. When we came to the end of the final tunnel, I tried to talk to him. "Do you think we should still

go to Deyrolle?" I asked, even though it had been my request. "It's a lot of death in one day."

"You've been begging me to go and here I am, so we should do it now." He said it as if he might not be coming back.

He realized the finality of his comment and tried to make light of it. "Also for inspiration."

"Inspiration for what?"

"Our papier-mâché babies."

"We could go to the zoo."

"No, if we are creating mythological creatures in the basement we need to look at these beasts up close, to be as accurate as possible."

"Accurate to what?"

"Their animal halves."

"May I buy a beetle pinned in a little black box there?" I asked. I had always wanted one.

"Do you have any money?"

"No."

"What about from babysitting?" I babysat the four Southern children who lived in Le Vésinet. They were all blond, under the age of five, and completely wild. I made fifty francs, about ten dollars an hour, to prevent them from killing each other.

"I spent it all on the magazines I bought last week. American *Vogue* costs the equivalent of two hours of work."

"Then, no bug. You have to live within your means."

I followed my father into the car and slammed the door.

"We need to go," he said without warning after looking at something in the pocket within his blazer. "I mean we can't go to Deyrolle." He kept glancing down as he started the engine.

"Why all of sudden?"

"I need to go into the office."

"Can I come?"

"No."

o   o   o

The long-awaited field trip had arrived, and for whatever reason, spelunking was part of the activities our class was to enjoy during our sojourn in the French countryside. We were instructed to wear clothes that could be thrown out when the day was over and to show up on time at the base of the mountain.

There was little instruction before we entered the cave, except for how to turn on our headlamps. In the first minutes, we saw three bats and countless stalagmites and stalactites. This was in the larger part of the cave, where we could all stand up and see one another, as well. After walking for half an hour, we came to a small opening in a wall. "You are each to crawl through this hole," the instructor said in French. "It will be tight the rest of the way, just breathe and do not worry." With that we started to enter the hole headfirst, lights beaming. I stuck my head in just as Charlotte's feet slid forward. There was cool mud everywhere, and I had to pull my body up and into the tunnel. It was suffocating, and I couldn't extend my arm or leg anywhere but forward. We slithered until we came to a larger opening where we were able to stand again. As far as I could tell, no one made an official count to make sure everyone had made this leg of the journey. Then, it was a short drop down another hole via a black rope and into another tiny tunnel, which smelled of mildew and something else. Someone yelled, "Stop."

"What's up?" the instructor asked.

"He's stuck."

"Who?"

We all knew who it was. Our Thai prince was too round for the tunnel. Someone should have thought about this sooner. We were all going to die in this cave in the South of France, become legendary like Lascaux.

"He's moving!" And then we were off again, slinking around, eager to get out into the open air.

The following day there was to be no more outdoor sports, only a sightseeing trip to Vézelay.

We'd left the hostel where we were all staying to go visit the cathedral and surrounding town. After we were dropped at the center of the village, we were allowed to wander for three hours. This free time was standard for such trips. The same had happened when we'd gone to Avignon last year. Everyone took advantage of the hours differently. Jake and Raees usually went to a café to smoke, and sometimes I or Charlotte and Sarah— never both at once—joined them. Natalie would go shopping for souvenirs. I would often walk around alone with my *camera*.*

---

* The world is distorted or clarified through various lenses, seen differently according to the glass's definition. When the microscope was invented around 1590, it became easy to distinguish between fairies and fruit flies. Before the camera's creation, people often thought insects were magical creatures. Science allowed them to marvel at real gossamer wings. The optic discoveries of the Victorian age then effectively changed the way humanity saw the world. Even before these advancements, Belgian magician Étienne-Gaspard Robert, also called "Robertson," was known for his stage antics, creating phantasmagoria

I loved going into the old churches—the Gregorian chants eerily pumped into the cavernous halls, the stale air, the candles lit for loved ones. I was obsessed with *relics** and reliquaries, the

---

using projectors, screens, and smoke. He took over the ruined Couvent des Capucines near Place Vendôme and turned it into a macabre theater where he would pretend to channel Rousseau and Voltaire by projecting their images on his fanciful stage. Robertson suggested the French use enormous mirrors to torch the British navy (an idea they declined).

During this time there was also a penchant for animated paintings, à la Dorian Gray, moving statues, and other diversions of this nature. These amusements were the precursors to the earliest cinema from the likes of the Lumière brothers.

---

* The cult of relics raged during the Middle Ages, when the blood and body parts of holy men and women became venerated objects, their location—be it church or temple—the place of pilgrimage for thousands of believers seeking to be closer to their god. Christian examples are among the most well known, but such objects exist for other religions, such as the Buddha's left canine housed in the Temple of the Tooth in Kandy, Sri Lanka, or Muhammad's footprint among the treasures of Topkapi Palace. In Christianity, relics include the Shroud of Turin, thought to be the cloth that covered Jesus Christ at his death (it is said that photographs in negative show the outline of his face) and splinters of the crucifixion cross, known as the True Cross. The Sudarium

idea that part of an ancient body or blood could be housed in a beautiful, little monument for future pilgrims.

That night, back at the hostel, we were supposed to have a canteen. I thought a canteen was a cafeteria, but I soon learned it was a dance. Everyone was excited about the event, although the boys feigned indifference as they drank behind the rooms. We were all allowed wine at dinner, and they'd made friends with the busboy, who gave them full bottles on the sly.

I couldn't decide what to wear. A dress might be trying too hard, so I settled on a pair of two-tone shorts and a black T-shirt with my scarab necklace. I had also found a little turquoise bead

---

of Oviedo is a remnant of bloodstained material believed to be from Jesus's death as well. The Sainte-Chappelle once held the crown of thorns, which is now within Notre Dame in Paris. There is also the Catholic phenomenon of the Incorruptibles, bodies of saints that when exhumed remain intact and smell of flowers. The body of Saint Bernadette, the visionary of Lourdes, did not decay after thirty years underground. Another Incorruptible, Saint Catherine Labouré, now lies in a glass coffin at 140 rue du Bac, the same street where one finds Deyrolle full of its preserved animals. Relics may also be objects such as a chalice or personal effects, like Saint Bernadette's umbrella from her trip to Nièvres. All are physical evidence of the divine.

on one of my nighttime outings and strung it on a black cord to make a choker. I decided my Adidas Samba sneakers were most appropriate with the outfit. Then, I saw Charlotte.

She was wearing jean cutoffs with high-heeled glitter jelly shoes and a concert T from when the Red Hot Chili Peppers had come to Paris. There was a black bandanna rolled up and tied around her neck. She looked sexy and insouciant. Her blond hair was messy and down, falling around her shoulders. All the girls were meant to meet at the bottom of the hostel to walk together to the room where the canteen was to be. I watched from the window and then followed a few paces behind. When we arrived, we were met with the flashes of a dizzying strobe light someone had brought along for the occasion. Without warning, the music stopped and ten of the guys ran into the room, two with guitars. One started strumming the cords to Nirvana's "Rape Me" as the others started singing the PG version they'd written at the café earlier that day.

"Eat Grapes" was the refrain.

At the end of the parody number everyone applauded, the teachers the loudest. The social studies teacher, Mr. Goose, couldn't stop laughing. The room was silent, as he was DJ for the evening and was fumbling for the next song. I knew what was coming. Charlotte had started to move in the direction of Raees, and the other girls had followed her lead to look for dance partners. Guns N' Roses' "November Rain" began to play, and I watched Raees put his hands around Charlotte's waist. She balanced her wrists on his shoulders. Everyone had found someone; there was no one left. Even Jake had already coupled with the new girl from New York City.

Nobody noticed as I walked off. There was a path marked with neon orange spray paint that led into the woods. I followed the markers to a clearing filled with moss-covered logs. As I lay flat facedown on the ground, I could feel the moisture seep into my clothes. I closed my eyes and flipped over. This night walk would end differently from the others. I was the odd number, on my back, staring up until my eyes crossed and everything appeared mirrored, like the picture within a *kaleidoscope.*

---

* Scotsman David Brewster grew up in Inchbonny, where he spent time with a young blacksmith, James Vetch, who taught him about telescope mirrors. Fascinated by optics, Brewster, an inventor and philosopher, continued to explore the field only to discover in 1816 he could create beautiful patterns with lace, beads, and glass pieces reflected

My legs were spread to each side and my hands overhead so that my back arched toward the sky. I started to cry quietly at first. In the stillness of the night, I could make out the song that had started to play back at the dance, one of my favorites: Bush's "Glycerine." Then I felt my chest lift and my stomach turn. I hadn't eaten anything all day, for a few days. Not eating was a nice distraction. There was nothing to vomit, even though my body tried.

---

in many folds. The invention of the kaleidoscope caused a sensation that, sadly for Brewster, led to immediate copies and mass production of the marvelous little toy, owing to an improperly worded patent. What is most alluring about the kaleidoscope, and perhaps what contributed to its great popularity in the nineteenth century, is the human draw to symmetry—in beautiful faces, flowers, and other phenomenon.

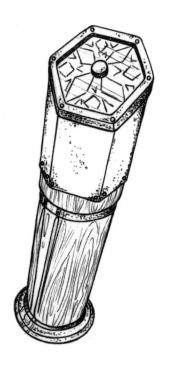

Le Vésinet

I was surprised the bathroom mirror didn't break when I threw the razor. It was one of those disposable models with a hot-pink handle and three tiers of blades from a drugstore in America. I wanted the glass to break, but instead, the square mirror of the medicine cabinet was swiped shiny and clear where the plastic hit the foggy glass. A pump of *pamplemousse*-scented body wash lay on the floor bleeding shower gel, next to the toilet. I was lying there with my left leg hanging over the edge of the white basin, my right leg bent backward violently shaking, beating the tile wall. My hands were trembling. I couldn't open my eyes. They were so wet, red, and raw from crying.

It had started with that telling pressure, that feeling when the tears start to pool behind my nose. I had tried to suck in air an even number of times, as if to be cured by my own twisted numerology. The rising sensation came too fast and two became three and then six became seven and then I knew what would happen. It reminded me of Cécile in the movie version of *Bonjour Tristesse*, except she liked odds until Anne died in the seventh accident on that corner in the South of France. Françoise Dorléac, Grace Kelly, and Albert Camus died in car crashes, too. I knew that fact but not much else about them. What was the point? It had been three days since I'd eaten anything.

The teenage Cécile had been similarly bothered by cloying thoughts that made her try to push them out of her mind with games of odds and evens. I was momentarily proud of my own intelligence with this reference, inflated at a moment when everything else was overblown too. Perhaps the reason Cécile would never do her philosophy homework was because she knew that old Pascal's theories on distraction would explain away her silly diversions and then they wouldn't work anymore. She didn't go for religion but instead for sexual desire and counting until it didn't work anymore. I would never have the boy. I didn't have the South of France, either.

Only Le Vésinet.

So far from anything.

I didn't know how to have fun, how to look forward when there wasn't much to see. Ever since the school trip, when they had found me in the woods lying in clear vomit, and word had gotten around school, things became worse. You'd think girls would be nicer if they knew you'd had a breakdown, but the opposite happened. They taunted me daily with their laughter and stares, which always made the tears come, even if quietly. I tried to hold my feelings in, but I knew that they saw. They could see me start to hyperventilate as I sucked air in and my chest lifted, the beats between breaths getting shorter and shorter. And it was more evidence that they were right about me.

In the shower, I found that the tears went away. They blended in with the running water, which made everything seem more normal. I didn't like seeing my naked body in the light. It was all boyish and ugly. The magazines and models were only fantasy, another diversion. I'd never get there, to that place where I would feel beautiful and loved and fine, or even pretty and just okay. I was left to think and remember, think and remember, until it drove me mad and into the shower. Always into the shower, avoiding the mirror, allowing it to fog. I would stay under the water for so long that my hands would prune as they did when I was a child, happy in my bath.

This time, I'd been in the bathroom for hours. At some point, I'd knocked down the convertible showerhead. It had undulated on its articulated cord and hit me in the face before falling down and spraying water everywhere. I didn't care. I counted seven of its slams, before it lay still.

I was numb, starving, and shivering, naked on the shower floor, my head propped against the wall I had kicked until my heels hurt. Everything was wet. I couldn't breathe, the air thick with humidity from the steam. The window to the street was too high up and far away for me to open it and let in some fresh air. I tried to get up and fell backward. Then, I managed to stand and turn off the water. I made it to the sink before I fell forward, my head creating a half-moon on the door of the medicine cabinet next to where the razor had hit earlier. I don't remember much after that.

New York

Fall 2009

I hadn't seen Jake since years ago, when we had met at the Guggenheim before going away to college. I remember only one scene from the encounter: spinning around the museum's spiraling staircase with our arms spread like wings. When we reached the ground floor, we ran out as fast as we could before anyone could have a word with us about our behavior. I don't recall talking about France, because I don't think we really did. I remember just twirling with abandon. He had been the only one to understand my kind of crazy. I wouldn't see him again for five years.

o   o   o

Our second meeting was in Manhattan at the Odeon restaurant. Jake looked the same as he had in France, though a little taller, a little more handsome, but the same sandy hair and flashing eyes. Except more than ten years of maturity had lent him the calm that had eluded us both back then. He seemed at ease with himself and happy with his work in filmmaking. I couldn't understand why I hadn't appreciated his attention as much as I should have when we were young, which meant I'd grown up as well. Instead of fixating romantically on Raees, I should have accepted and cultivated my friendship with Jake—that's really all it was. Raees was no longer tall and he was an art dealer, having left behind dreams of working in cinema.

"If you'd have asked me then what you'd end up, I thought you'd be a hippie, a free spirit poet," Jake said as he picked apart a piece of bread. "You were like a flower child obsessed with *butterflies*[*]— you had this really funny handwriting and drew insects on everything. You had a very beautiful spirit. You were strange, but it didn't really bother me. I thought it was endearing. You weren't like

---

[*] Just as Egyptian tombs and medieval catacombs were ravaged for treasure, butterflies are also victims of contemporary black market smugglers like Hisayoshi Kojima, the Japanese-born king of a vast multimillion-dollar ring of insect poachers. They were two Queen Alexandra's Birdwing butterflies ordered by an undercover agent that led to Kojima's eventual capture. The species is the largest in the world, with a yellow body and mint-and-black-colored wings sometimes reaching almost a foot in width.

the other girls, and they definitely didn't like you."
He laughed. "Sorry. You know what I mean. It
seems as though you're doing well now."

"Thank you."

"How's your family?" he asked.

"Fine. I don't see them very often. My brother
loves the outdoors and spends much of his time
working in Vermont or Colorado."

"What does he do?"

"Disaster relief–something, or so he says. I
think he actually works with my father," I said.

"I remember your father did something
strange?"

"He says it was 'international business,' 'con-
sulting,' IBM, maybe. I think Sophie's dad said
the same thing. They both went to work in La
Défense at this building you had to enter through
Star Wars–like capsules."

"I bet he was a spy, like Raees's mom." Jake had
sensed my childhood hunch about my father's pro-
fession without my ever explaining any details to
him. "She once told us she worked for the Dutch
National Science Foundation, the DNSF. We were
like 'What the fuck's the DNSF?' Whenever we
hung out at Raees's place it was always a little
freaky. There were these Russian icons with gold-
lined eyes. I think they were painted in some sort

of wax technique. Raees's mom always warned us about smoking around them. I swear, one started to melt once when he lit a cigarette too close. Freaky. We thought maybe we could sell a couple on the black market," Jake said, laughing. "Whenever we went out she'd warn us to 'Watch out for wild women.' Everyone's parents were interesting. Do you remember when I didn't come to school for a little while?"

"Yeah, I never knew what happened. No one seemed to know. You just reappeared one day. I remember the teachers whispering. Considering you were my boyfriend, I thought you'd share if you wanted me to know."

Jake laughed.

"My mom woke me up one morning and said we were going away and I couldn't tell anyone. We were going to take the train to find my dad in Nice. He'd gotten a call from the CRS. They were like a special branch of the French government like the FBI.

"They'd told him, 'You need to get out of Paris for a while.' They'd intercepted a threat to an American executive at an American bank. 'We will let you know when you can return. Go as far away as you can, but stay in France and check into the hotel under a different name. We'll find you and contact you when it's safe to come back.'

"So, we stayed in a bed-and-breakfast in Nice."

"Wasn't that bizarre?"

"I don't know; it was normal. We were there with other kids too. They had thought my father was the most at risk, as he worked for United Bank of America. I guess if you were a terrorist you'd choose that over Chase? Anyway, after ten days passed, we received a call.

" 'The threat has been neutralized' was all they said."

"That's so crazy. My father was gone most of the time. My only vivid memories from back then are of what happened when he would come home. I forget almost everything that happened after I lost it."

"Lost it?" Jake asked.

"Yeah, I was severely depressed about a year before we moved back to the States. My mother found this American doctor in Paris that I used to see each week. I didn't let anyone help me until I decided to get better on my own. My recovery was faked when we returned to New York after my father's assignment. I tried to be normal, all-American: played lacrosse, dated football players, wore jeans. No one bought it, least of all myself. Every time I try too hard it falls flat. I had to finally accept I was different and figure how to get through the world alone this way. There was no cure. I never actually got better."

"To be honest, I had no idea."

"No?" I asked.

"It's true. Like I said before, you were this beautiful spirit. What may be off is your point of view. Most of us were alone a lot. I got a lot of teenage stuff out of my system over there. We had so much freedom. Raees and I would just go out and get wasted. We drank and smoked, and then when I moved back, there wasn't any desire for any of that partying anymore. By the time I got to prep school, it was like I had done all that stuff. We'd all grown up alone and so fast."

South of France

Sometime around 2010

Will was lying with his book on the bed, his back to me and my back to the Mediterranean Sea.

"Where are you going?" he asked, feeling me lift off the bed and toward the door.

"To walk around."

"Do you want me to come with you?"

"No."

We had arrived an hour ago from the Nice airport. I knew I would become restless in the hotel room. From the moment we landed, I felt uneasy. There had never been a Will when I had been living in France over ten years ago, and it felt strange to have his comfort in a place I had only known alone. Still, it wasn't Paris. I wasn't prepared for that yet.

I had nearly gagged when we arrived at the airport, on the walk down the clinical white border to customs. Neither Will nor I said a word. There was a small queue, because of a dirty-looking man holding up progress. A woman in a pressed blue shirt and ill-fitting black pants had unzipped his suitcase to find a disgusting pile of rotting black *pods* * that reminded me of the ones I had collected when I was young, as they fell off the trees with the change of seasons. She was lifting them up one by one with a silver caliper. Another agent was ushering people along. I couldn't help but stare backward, causing my duffel bag to fall off my shoulder. Will picked it up.

"What is that?" I asked, craning my neck. Will was carrying all of our luggage.

"I don't know, but they don't want it in France. And I don't blame them," he said. I imagined someone must have once said the same of me. Even though Will and I had been together for a few years, I was still afraid to explain to him in

---

* In Inuit lore, the creation of man began with a raven coming forth from the darkness to create an enormous pea pod. The bird didn't intend for anything extraordinary to come from it, so it was quite surprised when a man emerged fully formed, splitting the seedling's skin. The two were equally perplexed to find each other, and the raven, realizing the man's hunger, set about to find him something to eat. The bird returned with berries and soon created beasts, as well as a woman to be the companion for this new being. As pods continued to bear seeds and fruit, perhaps this is why pea pods became lucky gifts in English country courtship, said to bring love and fertility.

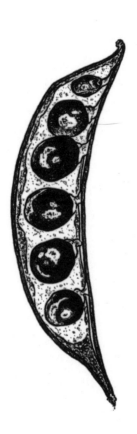

particular what had happened when I was thirteen. Everyone knows these sorts of conditions never fully go away. I'd presented my childhood as full of whimsy and mystery rather than sadness, so much so that I'd started to believe this version as well.

We found our way quickly to the car that would take us on to Monaco. I had a special love for the tiny country, and it hadn't escaped me that once we arrived, we'd no longer technically be in France. Some of my best memories of my grandparents weren't memories at all, rather imagined scenes pieced together from photographs and stories. A bon vivant, my grandfather was a Sinatra-singing businessman and actor who loved to take my grandmother away from Massachusetts to Monte Carlo. During the evenings, she'd dress up in a long Yves Saint Laurent skirt and blouse, according to pictures, and smoke, always with her gold bangles, one for every child, on her right arm (I wear them now; my mother gave the five to me when I was in college) and a long, brown plait of hair down her back. She was a beauty, and he was a charmer who liked to sing songs from Old Blue Eyes in the kitchen, at parties, or between puffs of a smoke. He once told me about eating dinner next to Grace Kelly on one of their trips to Monaco.

On the wall of my first apartment in New York, I'd hung a picture of my grandfather looking out of a boat with a drink on the rocks in one hand and a cigarette in the other, a windswept American flag behind him. He is wearing a sweater with red-and-blue stripes at the neckline, and his hands are flung upward, against the backdrop of the Mediterranean. On the same wall was another picture, of my mother on the runway of a tiny airport standing next to her younger brother, who was nearly a foot taller than she was. They are about to board a small plane to meet my grandfather and grandmother at their house in Saint Martin. My mother seems a little sad and lonely. This image sometimes reminds me of how ungrateful I'd been growing up. How hard France must have been for my mother too. I think my grandmother's sense of aesthetics and entertaining style influenced my mother. But they didn't talk much.

o   o   o

That night in Monaco, I left the hotel wearing a silk nightgown with Will's coat jacket thrown over it. No one seemed surprised by a woman in a slip dress. Night walks were still my favorite things to do in foreign places—a micro example of France translating into the source of my sensibility—and

Will was used to such erratic behavior. I think it intrigued him, along with the story of my childhood. That was one of the side effects of being "different" that I hadn't counted on: it made men curious.

When I was young, I thought that the perfect woman was Hemingway's Lady Brett Ashley. Then I discovered there were some men who liked a little torture translated into madness—and Ashley may not have been so sane after all. "She's crazy" sometimes meant she took every kind of passion too far. Beyond Miller, Casati, and Castaing, I'd recently read about *Nancy Cunard** and her rebellion against the aristo-expectations of her

---

* Shipping heiress Nancy Cunard was born in 1896 into an English life of finery. The slim beauty chose, however, to reject this lineage in favor of escaping to Paris's Left Bank and the pulsating world of surrealism and Dada, as started by the likes of her lover Louis Aragon. She found her inner circle among men like Man Ray, Ernest Hemingway, Ezra Pound, and James Joyce while being ostracized from the society she left behind. She would go on to establish the Hours Press, which would publish the impressive nearly nine-hundred-page *Negro: An Anthology*. Cunard was known for her affair with black pianist Henry Crowder, her work against fascism, and her armfuls of African bangles. In 1965, she succumbed to mental illness and passed away in Paris.

English mother. Like Miller, she captivated artistic men. There was also the French-adopted American *Jean Seberg*,* once married to diplomat and writer Romain Gary. He divorced the established Lesley Blanch for Seberg, a high-stakes trade winning him a partner with youth and instability. Miller, Casati, Cunard, and Seberg all dealt with depression toward the end of their lives, which meant it'd been hiding all along. I obsessed over their stories, searching for evidence to support the happy ending of my own.

Will once said, "I'll never be bored a day in my life with you." He'd tried to pass the backhanded compliment off as a joke, but I knew he meant every word. My problems had been behaving

---

* Like Miller, Jean Seberg was from a small American town and later found herself French. She was born in 1938 in Marshalltown, Iowa, and eighteen years later, out of countless hopefuls, she was cast as Joan of Arc in Otto Preminger's film of George Bernard Shaw's *Saint Joan*. She went on to become known for her roles in *Bonjour Tristesse* and as the *New York Herald Tribune*–hawking American ingenue in *Breathless*. Early in her career she expressed her sympathy for Sagan and her premature fame. Seberg committed suicide in 1979, allegedly prompted by an FBI conspiracy. Ten years later, her first husband, Romain Gary, would do the same.

themselves as they had when I was very young, though there was always the chance of resurrection. France was the trigger the first time around.

I continued walking, pulling Will's blazer down on my shoulders. It had taken years for me to see the childish selfishness of my behavior and childhood depression, but also the innocence of it. My poor parents had suffered because I'd been sad and spoiled with their love. I often thought about how my mother had to take care of herself as a teenager and how this led to her resilient and optimistic spirit. I hadn't meant to be unappreciative. I never would have believed I would have found someone to love, to take back to France with me. And I had left him alone in a hotel room, our first night away.

There was a café at the end of the path, which was still open. I sat down.

"Can I help you, my butterfly?" the waiter asked, looking up and down the length of my dress.

"A tea, please."

"Where are you from, you speak such good French?" he said. I felt an odd sensation when he brushed by my arm to pick up the menu.

"New York," I lied.

"Ah, New York, a little beauty from New York." He turned away from the table.

When he returned, he was carrying a bright yellow ceramic cup of hot water and a *tea bag** with EARL GREY written in white letters on a navy blue paper square. "I brought you English tea," he said, "because you are English girl." He was confusing ethnicity with language. I shook my head.

"You don't like it?"

"No, I am American," I said in French, "not English." I used the word that described someone from England, rather than the tongue.

"Ah, I see. We do not have any American tea."

"It's okay," I said lifting the cup. He brought over some milk and sugar.

"You are alone here?"

"No." I smiled with apologetic eyes and pulled on the lapel of Will's oversize blazer, surprised at my confidence.

I drank my tea in silence, allowing my mind the

---

* About a hundred years ago, when tea importer Thomas Sullivan received his usual shipment of sea cargo from India and China, he decided he didn't want to pay for the standard tin boxes to send out samples to his vendors. Instead Sullivan measured tiny amounts of tea in silk sachets, which retailers unwittingly placed directly into hot water to brew a cup. Thus, tea bags were serendipitously created. Silk became too expensive, and soon gauze and other materials were used for the disposable sachets.

rare freedom to wander back to Le Vésinet, and then asked for the check.

"It is on me," he said. I did not refuse him.

Paris

Sometime around 2010

I have a funny relationship with Paris taxi drivers. We either instantly bond because they recognize I speak French with a native accent, or we get in terrible fights. The latter happened when I told the driver to take me to rue du Mont-Thabor and he thought I had said rue de Montalembert. When we arrived at the wrong destination, I asked him to please take me to the right spot. I explained that he had misunderstood the address. He shook his head and refused to move the car. I told him I'd pay whatever he wanted. He told me it was out of principle and that I should get out and walk. I sat in the car for half an hour and he still refused to drive me, which left me no choice but to call another taxi. I waited for the second taxi to arrive while sitting in the first.

I decided it was best to call a driver for the following day of appointments and shows. Paris was harder to navigate with the traffic of everyone in town for the fashion collections. I too had come for this reason. Vanya was the name of the driver. He spoke with a thick Russian accent. I knew I'd understand his French better than his English. From the start, he had his own assumptions about me.

"You are from New York?" he asked as soon as I settled in the backseat. "So you know De Niro?"

"Robert De Niro?"

"Yes, yes."

"No, not really."

"I was in a film with him once. I am an actor, also high security."

"What do you mean?"

"I was shot three times once. I used to be in charge of the security surrounding the Eiffel Tower."

"That's a big job."

"Yeah, I know. One day a crazy man came with a gun and was threatening everyone, so we had a standoff. It happened at the southwest leg of the tower. He was about to shoot and I slid on the ground and grabbed his leg and then knocked his gun out of his hand."

"Oh my goodness."

"I then went to be bodyguard for movie stars, which is how I know De Niro. I worked on many movie sets. You know that guy who plays Bond?"

"Pierce Brosnan?" He shook his head. "Daniel Craig." He nodded.

"I was in that movie, they said they liked the way I looked and I played a bodyguard."

I giggled a little in response.

"What do you do?"

"I work in fashion."

"Are you a model?"

"No, a writer." He looked disappointed.

"You know Kate Moss?"

"Not really." He looked even more disappointed. "You have a boyfriend?"

I nodded.

"What does he do?"

"Oh, um, finance and a little film."

He got very excited. "He is film producer? Here, take my picture with your iPhone. Wait, actually give me your e-mail."

"Okay," I said. He handed me one of his cards and a pen, and I wrote down my e-mail.

"I will e-mail you my headshot and you give to your boyfriend and he can help give to casting agent. You know I play taxi driver in Julie Delpy's film. They like my look also for these tough spy movies." We were driving down the Champs-Élysées, past the theaters toward the Hôtel de Crillon and the obelisk in the Place de la Concorde. "We need to take a detour," he said.

"Why?"

"Too much traffic this way, trust me."

We drove down a few streets and stopped across from a line of people winding around the corner of a lovely stone building.

"What's that?" I asked.

"French people are curious. They like to see people they think are intelligent do stupid things." I realized he was referring to Jacques Chirac, who was awaiting trial. The bystanders looked like Eddie Vedder groupies waiting for Pearl Jam tickets.

"You aren't like this in America," he said.

I shook my head and stared out the window as the top of the *obelisk** on the Place de la Concorde

---

* How does one manage to transport a sixty-eight-foot high and nearly 250-ton piece of red granite from Egypt to New York, London, or Paris? The move happens with the aid of a series of deceptively primitive levers and machinery, much the same way the hulking obelisks were once created in ancient Egypt and carved with hieroglyphs celebrating Ramses II. It was in the early nineteenth century that Muhammad Ali of Egypt and Sudan gifted the two obelisks that guarded the Temple of Luxor to France. The first one arrived in 1833 and was moved three years later to the square where Louis XVI and Marie Antoinette had been guillotined at the turn of the century, the Place de la Concorde. New York's and London's own misnamed "Cleopatra's needles" (neither has a distinct link to the

queen) arrived at the end of the nineteenth century. The twin obelisk promised to Paris remained in Egypt until François Mitterrand, nearly one hundred years later, announced it should stay in its original country. In 1998, the French government gave their obelisk a special gift, a new gold chapeau, as somewhere in history it had lost its original cap.

came into sight. "We are almost there," Vanya said. "Will you need me tomorrow?" he asked.

"No, thank you. I have something else to do."

o　o　o

The following morning I called a cab to take me to Le Vésinet. I had intended to take the RER train, but it looked as though it would rain and Vanya was likely already dispatched.

"Rue Ampère, please," I said to the cabdriver as I got inside. "Le Vésinet. . . . Actually, can you take me to Les Ibis, instead, near the Palais Rose?"

"Okay," he said in English, completely uninterested in me. I fell asleep on our way.

"Mademoiselle, we are here," he said. I looked out the window and saw the rue Diderot *street sign**

---

* Abbé Grégoire was a controversial eighteenth-century figure—a Roman Catholic priest and ardent supporter of republican virtue, religious equality, and abolitionism. Inspired by the Philadelphia Quakers and the organization of Washington, D.C., he is known for his work to rename the Parisian streets postrevolution. "Each name ought to be the vehicle of a thought, or, rather of a sentiment that reminds citizens of their virtues and duties," he was quoted as saying. In 1989, his body was moved to the Panthéon in recognition of such forward-thinking ideals, though there was still resistance among certain Frenchmen.

before offering my credit card. "Have a nice time. I hope you get through on the other side." Perhaps he'd meant something else but hadn't known the proper English equivalent. I stepped out of the car onto the path to the Palais Rose's gold and black gates on the corner of Allée des Fêtes.

I didn't need to go any closer to the mansion. There was no longer someone looking at me through the window, and the swans had gone elsewhere. I knew the architecture by heart. So many times I'd lain awake alone in bed and imagined one of the Marchesa Casati's absurd theme parties playing out on the sprawling lawn covered in carpet and black candles. She used to have illuminated signs set up all the way from the bridge over the Seine to the Palais Rose to guide her guests. This was the same path she would take in her blue Rolls-Royce when she grew bored of Le Vésinet, which was often, and decided to go on treasure hunts for amusement. Her friend, photographer and diarist Cecil Beaton, recounted a story of the marchesa deciding she wanted to find an object in a certain shade of orange to relieve her boredom. My father would have liked this game but would have been unable to see it as evidence of the isolation of living in Le Vésinet. The marchesa is now long gone, relegated to bizarre, lost stories, much like my childhood.

As I walked away from the palace, I noticed there were four mushrooms clustered together at the edge of the road. I knew better than to try to pick one. I remembered how after our visit to the museum of natural history, my father never forced our agreement that I throw away the mushroom. It had stayed in my collection until we moved back to the States. Its shriveled little body was then lost somewhere along the way. My other objects and collections still existed, though they'd started to morph to represent real, critical, connected themes rather than random things. People were no longer classified like the deities of Greek mythology, or the tidy trays of insects at Deyrolle. I'd kept all the objects because they were evidence of the beauty in the unusual, not as empty souvenirs of France. I thought about meeting Will and laughing at all his jokes, thinking they were original material until someone said they were from *Seinfeld*. I'd missed that moment in American television culture, just as I'd missed growing in the States in favor of deceased women and lucky charms.

o   o   o

I was worried that I wouldn't know how to get back to our old house. I'd taken the walk so many times, though at night and so long ago.

"Excuse me, is this the way to rue Ampère?" I asked a man walking by.

He shook his head and pointed in the other direction. I didn't listen and walked past a green painted gate and a roundabout before taking two lefts and then a right. There it was: rue Ampère and a few meters down, our house. There was someone standing in the window of the upstairs bathroom. I stood there in the middle of the street and started to cry.

New York

Sometime in 2011

"I'm still the same," I said to my mother. We were sitting on a bench in Central Park. She took a drink from the paper coffee cup in her left hand as she watched a little boy run by. My mother had done everything to give Zach and me an upbringing unlike her own. Forced to be independent as a child, she wanted us to be able to rely on her. She'd come to visit me in Manhattan that afternoon, sensing I was relapsing into my old ways, to try to protect me from real complications, not the angsty delusions of Le Vésinet.

My mother put down the cup.

"You're selfish, Stephie, you don't think of how your actions affect others. I stopped sleeping that last year in France and I'd never had insomnia before."

"I know. I'm sorry. It all exploded on me last week. I'm sorry I haven't been to visit you. I thought the sooner I got away from what reminded me of France, I'd be cured. Only the opposite occurred. New people came into my life and I treated them like old friends, because I had none."

"People aren't going to understand your eager-ness. It's okay to be alone and patient. You have to trust."

"Trust what?" I asked.

"Things."

She lifted her coffee cup and pointed at a young boy carrying a *sailboat** and a long stick to push it through the pond. "He reminds me of your brother. Do you remember he used to sail boats in the bidet whenever we wouldn't take him to Les Ibis?"

"Yes."

"Have you talked to him recently?"

"No."

"He's been spending much of his time with

---

* William Faulkner found solace in the calm and civilized world of France far from his native Mississippi. He loved to sit in the Luxembourg Gardens and watch old men sail boats. "Think of a country where an old man, if he wants to, can spend his whole time with toy ships, and no one to call him crazy or make fun of him!" he once said. The plea-sures of these gardens was also not lost on Zelda Fitzger-ald, who in one of her letters recounts taking her daughter, Scottie, to play there. "When we were not in school," she recalled, "we would meet each other at the Luxembourg Gardens to sail the toy boats or ice skate at the grand palace or roll hoops. . . . It was a delightful time."

Blake restoring that old sailboat up at the house in Cape Cod." I had one real friend in college, and she and my brother had fallen in love. It was during a late-night conversation at university that Blake shared with me her own parallel childhood: her father was an oil executive and her family moved around the world from Texas to England, where a young Diana Spencer was her nanny, then to Jakarta in Indonesia. Years later she would know me so well, well enough to tell me, "You're a beacon for crazy people." I told her I wouldn't want it any other way, and she agreed, laughing. Blake and my brother had found each other because she too obviously had a taste for the gentle and borderline insane.

"Zach loved boats even when we were little."

"He still does, but they're real now."

Paris

"You catch up nicely," Adelaide said, sipping her espresso and staring back at me over the tiny café table. We'd been set up by a mutual French acquaintance who thought we should meet. She knew Adelaide from winters in Saint Moritz and summers in Ibiza. Somehow I ended up telling this stranger about not having many friends as a child, spending lonely months in Le Vésinet and weekends in Paris or Versailles. Her comment was flippant. She meant to say that now it seemed I have plenty of social engagements. I didn't care anymore about having many friends. "And what a lovely way to grow up." She pulled her blond hair back into a ponytail, patting the sides perfect. "You were living here around the time of the Concorde, non?" she asked.

I nodded.

"That was so amazing, you would sit down to a meal and arrive to Paris at dessert."

"I never went on it," I said. Some of my classmates had spoken of flying on the Concorde. When I'd mentioned it to my parents as an option for returning to New York during summer vacations, they'd laughed and asked, "When did you become so entitled?"

"Oh. Where are you staying now?" Adelaide said, switching the topic as she gestured to the waiter for the bill.

"L'Hôtel." I always stayed there, on the Left Bank in room 44, walking distance from where we were, at Café de Flore. The small hotel was once part of the palace of La Reine Margot and the last residence of Oscar Wilde.

"You don't have family here anymore?"

"No."

"No friends to crash with?"

"I'd rather not impose."

"I like your *bangles*,"* she said, changing the subject.

---

* The jeweler James de Givenchy once said that the luxury of a bangle is in that it is not precious: "You don't really care what happens to them; you can't care." No matter how precious the piece, the nature of a bangle is that it "bangs" into the bracelet next to it, often creating a sound that warns of its wearer's arrival. "Somehow I keep making them, even though they cannot be too fragile. A bracelet that is supple has a different purpose, it hugs the wrist." Still, there are always women who love to fill their arms with bangles, like Nancy Cunard and her arms of ivory, or Diana Vreeland. Givenchy recalls one of his uncle Hubert de Givenchy's

Alone was better than Adelaide.

o   o   o

That night at the hotel on rue des Beaux-Arts, I sat staring at my computer screen. It was 2 A.M. An hour earlier, I'd gone for one of my walks to nearby rue Jacob to pass by the site of Madeleine Castaing's shop, which had closed years ago, on the corner of rue Bonaparte. In its place was an autograph store run by her son. No one else had been outside at that hour, though it was a lovely July night. I peered into the window, looking for evidence of Castaing, an opaline glass or fading stripe wall, but there was not much to be seen from the street. So I turned back to the hotel. Even in the dark, it was easy to find, with the silver ram's head hanging over the door.

Once inside, I walked the four flights of leopard-carpeted stairs to my room. The walls of *chambre* 44 were painted mauve and hung with a delicate expanse of dark fabric suspended from rosettes. Black silk curtains hid some windows while others were draped in lace covered in thick velvet.

---

models, actress Capucine. "She often wore bangles, when we knew dinner was coming all you could hear was the bangles coming down the stairs, look at her such a beautiful girl."

The bed was beneath a violet canopy trimmed in deep mauve. My desk flipped open like a draw-bridge suspended by a gold chain.

I sat down, lit a *candle** smelling of roses and black currants, and opened my computer. There were e-mails to read, one message from an old boyfriend. He asked where I was. I said Paris. He knew L'Hôtel was where Oscar Wilde had died, and he also knew that I might fall apart in France.

"I picture you there. Always have. I can relate.

---

* Wax is an odd medium; it may cast molds of ephemera just as it may melt away when lit with fire. The ancient Fayum portraits on Coptic caskets were created using the encaustic technique, where wax is mixed with paint to produce lifelike colors. Ancient Grecian puppeteers also worked in wax, creating beautiful statues of little boys and fruits and vegetables. It was the eighteenth-century physician Philippe Curtius, Madame Tussaud's uncle, who first perfected the use of wax for models and miniatures, which he then taught to his niece. During the French Revolution, Tussaud would pull decapitated heads from heaps of carnage to create casts, as she did with Robespierre and Marie Antoinette. In 1777, she was invited to London by phantasmagoria expert, Paul Philidor to join in his show.

Wax bodies also served as a fetish for the bizarre. When entertaining, the Marchesa Casati is said to have set places for wax mannequins at dinner parties, including tragic figures like the murdered Baroness Mary Vetsera.

Not sure if something is consuming you but if so, stay the course and handle it within, take the bullet up to Mont St Michel and get through it. Go out on a limb here . . . YouTube the White Stripes' 'Jolene.' Do it Steph!!! It'll kill four minutes."

I Googled the video and listened to the song. It reminded me of our connection, of him. We were both a little dark, a little fucked-up. All we shared was a love for Hemingway and an odd understanding of each other, enough for him to know I should take a trip away from here.

Paris

More recently . . .

"You still want to go to the flea market, right?" Will asked, pushing his dark hair back behind his ears.

"Yes, we have to get there early, before everyone else."

"I didn't sleep last night, I was too worried about losing you to the Paris night. You worry me sometimes. Even I wouldn't walk around the city streets after hours." I laughed. He was six feet five, whereas I was elfin-looking, tall but frail. He might have been right to fear for my safety. The Parisian darkness had taken a few of my girls—Cunard, Seberg. Self-critical, introspective women court tragedy. They don't care about making friends.

Will knew there was potential for explosions with me and unpredictable, irrational behavior, but he stayed. Who knew how such extraordinary opposites could coexist—even love? Will clearly did not want to go to the flea market, but he understood it meant something to me.

"Steph, remember when we get there that there's a limit; we have to carry it all back." He wanted nothing to do with any sort of treasure hunt.

"You are so American," I said. He looked at me and smiled, shaking his head. A gesture he did often. I pushed him out the door.

It was easy to find a taxi at that early hour. The Parisian streets were empty except for a middle-aged man smoking a cigarette. Will nodded at him and raised his hand in hello. The taxi the hotel had called was waiting outside.

"Marché aux puces de la Porte de Vanves, s'il vous plaît," I said to the driver, who smiled at me in his rearview mirror. Will shook his head again. "They love you."

"They just don't know what to do with me. It doesn't make sense—American girl, French accent."

It took nearly an hour to get to the market. Every stall was already set up, and deals were being brokered on either side of the walkway.

"Isn't it amazing? Look!" I pointed to a group of objects set up nearby.

There were ceramic frogs, a silver-dipped lobster, two *scallop shells** on top of podiums, and giant, fragile branches of coral all spread on a purple carpet. "It will break when we try to bring it back," Will said before I could ask what he thought of the piece. We walked on and found a lady with a case of jewelry that held hundreds of *antique rings*†

---

* In French, scallops are known as *coquilles*, while their Latin name is *pecten*, meaning "comb." The ridged shell of the creature has come to represent the fervor of dedicated pilgrims making their way to Santiago de Compostela, known as the Way of Saint James. At the end of this Roman trade route, it is believed that when Saint James's body was being moved, a horse fell in the water and washed ashore unharmed and covered in scallops. The shells are not only symbolic but also practical in that pilgrims used them to scoop just enough food or water from offerings to sustain them along the journey. The scallop's primary enemy is the starfish, also parasitic sea creatures like barnacles or worms, which may weigh down the skilled swimmers.

† Human adornment began not only out of a need for beauty but also for charmed protection. The ancient Egyptians wore rings of cut stone scarabs attached to the finger with fine gold wire. Ancient Romans exchanged signet rings as symbols of brotherhood and allegiance, often carnelians or garnets carved with official seals used in correspondence. The sixteenth century brought memento mori jewelry, reminders of mortality. In the following century, rings also commemorated the lives of the beloved who had passed away, some bearing çiphers or hair of the lost. In

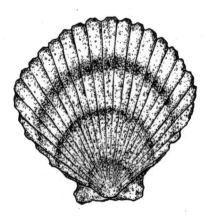

and a tiny bracelet made of five strands of coral

---

the eighteenth century, rings began to depict sepia painted urns or other morbid scenes. And along with new archaeological advances came the revival of interest in ancient Greece and Rome. The most privileged were able to obtain actual ancient stones. Sigmund Freud liked to present A.D. first-century Roman gifts to colleagues, while those with lesser means turned to James Tassie to make alternatives in paste known as "Tassies." Posy rings were named for the poems inscribed inside the band for one's beloved. Regards language also became popular, in which the first letter of a stone—often the same in French and English—would be used to spell out a message. *Regard* (ruby, emerald, garnet, amethyst, ruby, and diamond, as example). *Love* would be lapis lazuli, opal, vermeil (the ancient name for a type of garnet), and emerald.

beads with an antique diamond closure. "May I see that?" I asked her in French. She explained to me that though it dated back to the gaudy days of Napoléon III, it was understated and quite delicate. "Isn't it lovely?" I asked Will. "Or should we try to smuggle those coral branches?"

"I don't know about that. Remember the guy with the pods."

The old woman behind the jewelry stand looked at Will and asked him in French if he'd like to see any rings.

"No, thank you." he said. "Steph, we really don't need anything here. You're like a little kid, crazy over souvenirs."

"Fine. Then, I want to go somewhere where I can . . ."

"Oh no," he said smiling.

"I haven't even told you what it is—"

"I'm already sure it's hard to find."

"I know you're bored. Do you want to get something to drink?" I asked him.

"Sure." We walked to the nearest café and sat at a table out front.

The waiter came over, and Will spoke to him in English. "I'll have a beer and she'll have a tea. Do you have that flavor, er, that one with the *v*?"

I interrupted him. "*Verveine*." French for the herb verbena. The waiter nodded and left us alone.

"You need to calm down," Will said. "You claim to be sensitive to such small, pretty things, but you're giving yourself too much credit, you're obsessed with the past."

I started to get angry with him. He, like my mother, called out my selfishness.

"Why do you love these markets? We could be walking around Paris, enjoying the weather." The waiter came back with our drinks. He placed two primary blue–colored coasters on the round table and then set down the beer and teapot, cup, and saucer.

"You're okay," Will said. It wasn't a question. "You don't have to find all these random objects or read all these books to distract yourself from what's happening in your life. How many did you bring this time?"

I'd carried three with me and packed four hard-covers in my suitcase.

Will took a sip of his beer and looked out onto the sidewalk. "Do you want to eat something?" he asked with a little exasperation in his voice.

I nodded.

"The usual?"

Another nod. I couldn't speak.

He motioned to the waiter. "Haricots verts for her and a croque monsieur for me. Thanks."

"Vous voulez une autre bière?" Will shook his head.

"Don't think so much," he said, pushing back from the table to extend his legs. "You're missing everything."

The waiter brought two plates of food and set them on the table. I pushed aside the green beans. "Instead, I'll have a salad Niçoise."

My strangeness proved to be chemical, which meant objects would exist in and out of France, in and out of childhood. Chemistry can be played with, however; a catalyst here, the introduction of a new compound there—and neither necessarily of the medical variety. Science doesn't usually allow for matter to disappear, but rather for it to transform into something else altogether. Many of my enduring objects, both literal (the Nirvana CD, the skeleton key) and ephemeral (the ghost of a rotted mushroom and now-dead lilies of the valley) remain with my parents in Westchester. The latter I associate with each of them: the mushroom recalls my father, and the flower, my mother. Whenever I would visit from New York City, a trip similar in length to that from Paris to Le Vésinet, I risked falling backward to assigning the collection the same meanings. I began to research the lovely and unusual side of the list as a means to exorcise the past, to own the objects rather than the other way around. The whale's tooth and coral are in my Manhattan apartment, and the women sometimes appear, if only tangentially, in much of my writing. Once I replaced the space in my head with facts, figures, even the anxiety over crafting them into a narrative—a book!?—that would expose private pain to others in order to share a story, the inanimate objects were no longer important. Arguably it was rational maturity that drove me to recast them as fond memories rather than as voodoo talismans capable of conjuring up unwanted emotions. But even with this distance, I don't think we're ever too far from our younger selves. We still make mistakes. We continue to place value in new things (this can be good or bad), and we learn to live alone, on our own. This doesn't mean objects can't have worth, especially in their histories. Take, for example, the masking tape unicorn.

I hadn't seen my father in months when he called to let me know that he was retiring. I wasn't sure what that meant, as he also explained he'd stay contracted to certain overseas jobs at least for a little. During our talk, he also told me he and my mother would be moving to Cape Cod soon and that until then he would come to the city to see me for a weekly date.

That Wednesday the buzzer sounded, and I went to the panel on the wall to see who it was. My father was looking back at me smiling, making a funny face, knowing I'd be checking the camera before letting him in. He'd shaved his mustache sometime ago. It took him a few minutes to ride the elevator before it opened to my apartment, and he stepped inside.

"Stephie?" After pushing the button on the panel to call him up, I'd gone back to typing on my computer.

"Hey, Dad."

"I can't see you underneath all those books." I got up and went to him for a hug. He was carrying a large plastic case and two cardboard boxes. He took off the backpack he'd been wearing and placed it on the table, searching for something inside. "I brought you a gift."

"Really?" I asked.

"Yup, but first let's get something to eat, I'm starved."

I picked up my handbag and followed him, now wearing his backpack again, into the elevator and down to the street. New York's own version of a Parisian brasserie, Balthazar, was just around the corner. I took his arm as we walked over the cobblestones.

Once inside, we sat at my usual table tucked in the far left corner. A waiter with a French accent took our drink order.

"So, are you ready for your surprise?"

My father unzipped his bag and pulled out two rolls of blue masking tape. One had a slightly larger width than the other. He placed the circles side by side on the table.

"Masking tape?"

"Yup," he said, smiling. I was disappointed.

"You didn't buy that for me. You had the tape in your backpack."

He shook his head. "I got it for us. It's for your bell jars."

I had ordered seven large glass bell jars for a dinner party, and aside from flowers—anemones, ranunculus, and poppies—I had asked for his help in finding objects to capture inside. "I brought you an old film projector that your mom and I found at a flea market," he said, referencing the object he'd hauled upstairs in the case. "There's also an old *Life* magazine with the Beatles on the cover, a sea star, and some horseshoe crabs."

"Remember when we used to find them on the Cape, paint them, and you'd hang them on the wall?" I asked.

"I still have the one we spray painted silver for the beach house."

"I named that one Charybdis, after the sea

monster in Greek mythology. She was Poseidon's daughter." He smiled.

"So, what's the masking tape for?"

"You'll see."

We ate our lunch quickly and talked about Zach, Blake, and my mother. I asked my father if she was sleeping. He knew what I meant and assured me she was fine. I apologized to him again for all the trouble I continued to cause them.

When we arrived back at the apartment he tore into one of my magazines that had been stacked perfectly in a pile, all the spines aligned and arranged by date. He rolled the glossy pages into a head, four legs, a belly, a tail, even a single spiraling horn and started covering the horse made of paper with blue masking tape.

Acknowledgments

I am grateful to my editor, Maya Ziv, and to Billy Kingsland, Nicole Tourtelot, and David Kuhn for all their patience, hard work, and trust. Thank you, Julia Cheiffetz, for believing in me, and to Claire Austin for making it all happen. Claire, I still cannot understand how I found you. I am the luckiest girl in the world. Thank you, Laura McLaw Helms, for your kind help in searching magazine archives and special books.

For love and sharing our story, thanks to my parents, Robert and Sandra LaCava, and my brother, Garret LaCava. For love and letting me share their story, thanks to Helene, Ronald, and Alexandra Weiss and my husband, Bryan Weiss. I am also thankful to Ashley (Mooney) Cooper and Meredith (Faltermeier) Brewer for their unconditional friendship. Thank you to Caroline and Mary Robertson for being the earliest readers and supporters—Sweet Caroline, to think we met in a basement over a trash can. For their wisdom and brilliance, thanks to Indre Rockefeller, Aimee Mullins, Dodie Kazanjian, Ilana Darsky, Agathe Borne Rouffe, Chino Maurice, and Virginia Tupker.

I am so amazed at the work of Matthew Nelson and that he was willing to bring my objects to life in line drawings. Thank you also to Pamela Love. For his enduring spirit and vision, thanks to Henry Joost and to Mary Pittman Jones (Mrs. Jones) for her very special gifts. Thank you to Maggie Betts for listening and her knowledge of Yeats. For being awesome family, thanks to Shala Monroque and Jenke-Ahmed Tailly.

Notes

14   *"The great lesson of Dali's mustaches"*: Salvador Dalí and Philippe Halsman, *Dali's Mustache: A Photographic Interview* (Paris: Flammarion, 1994), 124.

19   *With kerosene readily available*: Donald Ridley P.E., personal interview, May 10, 2011.

24   *An agitated king*: Eric Monk, *Keys: Their History and Collection* (UK: Shire Publications, 1999), 16.

28   *He considered himself above all a scholar*: Terence K. McKenna et al., *The Sacred Mushroom Seeker: Tributes to R. Gordon Wasson* (Rochester, VT: Park Street, 1997), 49.

40   *"Some opali carry such a play"*: Allan Eckert, *The World of Opals* (New York: John Wiley and Sons, 1997), ix.

46   *In 2007, scientists found the most complete dodo skeletons*: "In Search of the Dodo," BBCKnowledge.com, BBC Corp., Web, Dec. 22, 2011, http://www.bbcknow ledge.com/nz/liberating/in-search-of-the-dodo.

53   *The blossom was also the namesake for Lily Bart*: Sharon L. Dean, *Constance Fenimore Woolson and Edith Wharton: Perspectives on Landscape and Art* (Knoxville: University of Tennessee Press, 2002), 156.

64   *Oscar Wilde wore a green scarab ring on his left hand*: Barbara Belford, *Oscar Wilde: A Certain Genius* (London: Bloomsbury, 2000).

64   *Charles Darwin was a devoted beetle collector*: Arthur Evans and C. L. Bellamy, *An Inordinate Fondness for*

Beetles (Berkeley: University of California Press, 2000), 137.

64 *The natural history museum in Paris houses the greatest collection of specimens*: Ibid., 22.

68 *At the end of her life she is said to have grown depressed*: Carolyn Burke, *Lee Miller: A Life* (New York: Alfred A. Knopf, 2005), xiii.

72 *Critics have said he chose this image as a means to hold on to innocence*: Michael Azerrad, *Come as You Are: The Story of Nirvana* (New York: Broadway, 2001), 182.

72 *It was the grunge band Mother Love Bone that was poised for stardom*: Jeff Kitts and Brad Tolinski, *Guitar World Presents Nirvana and the Grunge Revolution: The Seattle Sound: The Story of How Kurt Cobain and His Seattle Cohorts Changed the Face of Rock in the Nineties* (Milwaukee, WI: Hal Leonard in Cooperation with Harris Publications and Guitar World Magazine, 1998), 7.

85 *once documented, a human skull*: Max Bauer, *Precious Stones; a Popular Account of Their Characters, Occurrence, and Applications, with an Introduction to Their Determination, for Mineralogists, Lapidaries, Jewellers, Etc. with an Appendix on Pearls and Coral* (New York: Dover Publications, 1968), 601.

92 *The Allied governments encouraged daytime pajamas during the First World War*: Mary Schoeser, *Silk* (New Haven, CT: Yale University Press, 2007), 163–64.

92 *"They're the most adorably moon-shiny things on earth"*: F. Scott Fitzgerald and Zelda Fitzgerald, *Dear Scott, Dearest Zelda: The Love Letters of F. Scott and Zelda Fitzgerald*, Jackson R. Bryer and Cathy W. Barks, eds. (New York: St. Martin's Griffin, 2003), 14.

94   *"What the series' narration does best"*: Matt Zoller Seitz, "Never Trust a Narrator Who's Under 16," *New York Times*, October 30, 1994, 34.

96   *"I love how he's always leaning against stuff"*: "Pilot 1.1" *My So-Called Life: The Complete Series*. Dir. Scott Winant. BMG Special Product, 2002. DVD.

96   *"If you made a book about what really happened"*: Bruce Weber, "The So-Called World of an Adolescent Girl, as Interpreted by One," *New York Times*, August 25, 1994, C15/C20.

137   *Seberg committed suicide in 1979, allegedly prompted by an FBI conspiracy*: Jean Russell Larson and Garry McGee, *Neutralized, the F.B.I. vs. Jean Seberg: A Story of the '60s Civil Rights Movement* (Albany, GA: Bear-Manor Media, 2008).

147   *"Each name ought to be the vehicle of a thought"*: Priscilla Ferguson Parkhurst, *Paris as Revolution: Writing the Nineteenth-Century City* (Berkeley: University of California Press, 1994), 27.

154   *"Think of a country where an old man"*: Michael Grimwood, *Heart in Conflict: Faulkner's Struggles with Vocation* (Athens: University of Georgia Press, 2009), 32.

158   *"You don't really care what happens to them; you can't care"*: James de Givenchy, personal interview, Jan. 25, 2011.

160   *"She often wore bangles, when we knew dinner was coming all you could hear was the bangles coming down the stairs"*: James de Givenchy, personal interview, Jan. 25, 2011.

Bibliography

Books

Adams, W. H. Davenport. *Famous Caves and Catacombs, Described and Illustrated*. Lavergne, TN: Kessinger, 2009. Print.

Assouline, Pierre. *Deyrolle pour l'avenir*. Paris: Gallimard, 2008. Print.

Attenborough, David. *Amazing Rare Things: The Art of Natural History in the Age of Discovery*. London: Kales, 2009. Print.

Audas, Jane. "Mannequins." *The Berg Companion to Fashion*. Valerie Steele, ed. New York: Berg, 2010.

Azerrad, Michael. *Come as You Are: The Story of Nirvana*. New York: Broadway, 2001. Print.

Bagnoli, Martina, and Holger A. Klein. *Treasures of Heaven: Saints, Relics and Devotion in Medieval Europe*. London: British Museum, 2011. Print.

Balzac, Honoré de, and Napoleon Jeffries. *Treatise on Elegant Living*. Cambridge, MA: Wakefield, 2010. Print.

Bauer, Max. *Precious Stones; a Popular Account of Their Characters, Occurrence, and Applications, with an Introduction to Their Determination, for Mineralogists, Lapidaries, Jewellers, Etc. with an Appendix on Pearls and Coral*. New York: Dover Publications, 1968. Print.

Beaton, Cecil, and Richard Buckle. *Self Portrait with Friends:*

The Selected Diaries of Cecil Beaton, 1926–1974. London: Weidenfeld and Nicolson, 1979. Print.

Beaton, Cecil. *Self Portrait with Friends: The Selected Diaries of Cecil Beaton.* Richard Buckle, ed. London: Pimlico, 1991. Print.

———. *The Glass of Fashion.* London: Artillery Row, 1989.

Beckmann, Poul. *Living Jewels 2: The Magical Design of Beetles.* Munich: Prestel, 2007. Print.

Belford, Barbara. *Oscar Wilde: A Certain Genius.* London: Bloomsbury, 2000. Print.

Ben-Tor, Daphna. *The Scarab: A Reflection of Ancient Egypt.* Jerusalem: Israel Museum, 1993.

Bernstein, Jonathan, Grant Alden, and Jonathan Poneman. "Grunge Makes Good." *SPIN* Aug.–Sept. 1992: 52–67. Google Books. Web. Nov. 30, 2011. http://books.google .com/books?id=tAU7_ejzzoYC.

Berry, Sarah. *Screen Style: Fashion and Femininity in 1930s Hollywood.* Minneapolis: University of Minnesota Press, 2000. Print.

Bierbrier, Morris Leonard. *The Tomb-Builders of the Pharaohs.* Cairo: American University in Cairo Press, 1992. Print.

Bloom, Michelle E. *Waxworks: A Cultural Obsession.* Minneapolis: University of Minnesota Press, 2003. Print.

Blum, Dilys. *Shocking!: The Art and Fashion of Elsa Schiaparelli.* Philadelphia: Philadelphia Museum of Art, 2003.

Boire, Richard Glen, and Terence K. McKenna. *Sacred Mushrooms & the Law.* Berkeley, CA: Ronin, 2002. Print.

Boorstin, Daniel Joseph, and Ruth Frankel Boorstin. *Cleopatra's Nose: Essays on the Unexpected*. New York: Vintage, 1995. Print.

Bown, Nicola. *Fairies in Nineteenth-Century Art and Literature*. Cambridge: Cambridge University Press, 2001. Print.

Brewster, David. *The Kaleidoscope: Its History, Theory and Construction*. London: Van Cort Publications, 1858. Print.

Broer, Lawrence R., and Gloria Holland. *Hemingway and Women: Female Critics and the Female Voice*. Tuscaloosa: University of Alabama Press, 2002. Print.

Broglie, Louis Albert de, Patrick Mauriès, and Claude D'Anthenaise. *Nature Fragile: Le Cabinet Deyrolle*. Boulogne: Beaux-arts éd., 2008. Print.

Brown, Peter Robert Lamont. *The Cult of the Saints: Its Rise and Function in Latin Christianity*. Chicago: University of Chicago Press, 1982. Print.

Budge, E. A. Wallis. *Amulets and Superstitions*. 1930. Whitefish, MT: Kessinger Publishing, 2003.

———. *Cleopatra's Needles and Other Egyptian Obelisks: A Series of Descriptions of All the Important Inscribed Obelisks, with Hieroglyphic Texts, Translations, Etc*. New York: Kessinger, 2003. Print.

———. *The Mummy: A Handbook of Egyptian Funerary Archaeology*. New York: Cambridge University Press, 2010. Print.

Burke, Carolyn. *Lee Miller: A Life*. New York: Alfred A. Knopf, 2005. Print.

Burton, Maurice, and Robert Burton. *International Wildlife Encyclopedia*. New York: Marshall Cavendish, 2002. Print.

Byers, Michele, and David Lavery. *Dear Angela: Remembering My So-Called Life.* Lanham, MD: Lexington, 2007. Print.

Campbell, Joseph, and Bill D. Moyers. *The Power of Myth.* New York: Doubleday, 1988. Print.

Campbell, Susan. *A History of Kitchen Gardening.* London: Frances Lincoln, 2005. Print.

Chansigaud, Valérie. *Histoire de L'illustration naturaliste: Des Gravures de la Renaissance aux films d'aujourd'hui.* Paris: Delachaux et Niestlé, 2009. Print.

Chattman, Jon, and Rich Tarantino. *Sweet 'stache: 50 Badass Mustaches and the Faces Who Sport Them.* Foreword by John Oates. Illustrated by Brett Underhill. Avon, MA: Adams Media, 2009. Print.

Chisholm, Anne. *Nancy Cunard: A Biography.* New York: Penguin, 1981. Print.

Chisholm, Hugh, ed. "Thrones." *The Encyclopædia Britannica: A Dictionary of Arts, Sciences, Literature and General Information.* 11th ed., vol. 26. Cambridge: Cambridge University Press, 1911. 891–92. Google Books. Web. Dec. 14, 2011.

Cline, Sally. *Her Voice in Paradise.* New York: Arcade Publishing, 2004. Print.

Cocteau, Jean, and Pierre Chanel. *Past Tense, Volume II: Diaries.* San Diego: Harcourt Brace Jovanovich, 1988. Print.

Cocteau, Jean. *Past Tense: Diaries.* London: Methuen, 1990. Print.

———. *Souvenir Portraits: Paris in the Belle Epoque.* Paragon House Publishers, 1990.

The Collector; Containing Articles and Illustrations, Reprinted from The Queen *Newspaper, of Interest to the Great Body of Collectors, on China, Engravings, Glass, Needlework, Pictures and Embroidery, Lace, Old Silver, Old Books, and Prints, Etc.* London: Horace Cox, 1907. Print.

Colson, Jean. *Paris: Des Origines à nos jours*. Paris: Vision, 2007. Print.

Conway, D. J. *Crystal Enchantments: A Complete Guide to Stones and Their Magical Properties*. New York: Random House, 2000.

Coumbe, Clement W. "Chair." *Encyclopedia Americana: A Library of Universal Knowledge*. 1918. Google Books. Web. Dec. 11, 2011.

Cox, Carolyn. "Beards and Mustaches." *The Berg Companion to Fashion*. Valerie Steele, ed. New York: Berg, 2010.

Cox, Ian H. *The Scallop: Studies of a Shell and Its Influences on Humankind*. London: "Shell" Transport and Trading, 1957. Print.

Cranz, Galen. *The Chair: Rethinking Culture, Body, and Design*. New York: W. W. Norton, 1998. Print.

Crary, Jonathan. *Techniques of the Observer: On Vision and Modernity in the Nineteenth Century*. Cambridge, MA: MIT Press, 1995. Print.

Crofton, Ian. *Brewer's Cabinet of Curiosities*. London: Orion, 2006. Print.

Cutsem, Anne Van, and Mauro Magliani. *A World of Bracelets: Africa, Asia, Oceania, America from the Ghysels Collection*. Milan: Skira, 2002. Print.

Dalí, Salvador, and Philippe Halsman. *Dali's Mustache: A Photographic Interview*. Paris: Flammarion, 1994. Print.

Dean, Sharon L. *Constance Fenimore Woolson and Edith Wharton: Perspectives on Landscape and Art*. Knoxville: University of Tennessee Press, 2002. Print.

Deas, Lizzie. *Flower Favourites: Their Legends, Symbolism and Significance*. London: Allen, 1898. Print.

Dezallier D'Argenville, Antoine-Joseph, Veronica Carpita, Rainer Willmann, and Sophia Willmann. *Shells-Muscheln-Coquillages*. Hong Kong: Taschen, 2009. Print.

Dimant, Elyssa. *Minimalism and Fashion*. New York: Collins Design, 2010. Print.

Dixon, Ernest. "In the Land of Perfume." *The Wide World Magazine: An Illustrated Monthly of True Narrative, Adventure, Travel, Customs, and Sport*, Mar. 1908: 489–90. Google Books. Indiana University, Aug. 31, 2009. Web. Dec. 9, 2011.

Donnelly, Honoria Murphy, and Richard N. Billings. *Sara and Gerald: Villa America and After*. New York: Holt, Rinehart and Winston, 1984.

Eckert, Allan. *The World of Opals*. New York: John Wiley and Sons, 1997.

Evans, Arthur V., and C. L. Bellamy. *An Inordinate Fondness for Beetles*. Berkeley: University of California Press, 2000. Print.

Evans, Joan. *A History of Jewellery, 1100–1870*. New York: Courier Dover Publications, 1989.

Ferguson, Priscilla Parkhurst. *Paris as Revolution: Writing the Nineteenth-Century City*. Berkeley: University of California Press, 1994. Print.

Fitch, Noel Riley. *Sylvia Beach and the Lost Generation: A History of Literary Paris in the Twenties and Thirties*. New York: Norton, 1983. Print.

————. *Walks in Hemingway's Paris: A Guide to Paris for the Literary Traveler*. New York: Macmillan, 1992.

Fielding, Daphne Vivian. *Those Remarkable Cunards: Emerald and Nancy*. New York: Atheneum, 1968.

Fitzgerald, F. Scott. *Tender Is the Night*. New York: Charles Scribner, 1962. Print.

Fitzgerald, F. Scott, and Zelda Fitzgerald. *Dear Scott, Dearest Zelda: The Love Letters of F. Scott and Zelda Fitzgerald*. Jackson R. Bryer and Cathy W. Barks, eds. New York: St. Martin's Griffin, 2003. Print.

Ford, Hugh D., ed. *Nancy Cunard: Brave Poet, Indomitable Rebel, 1896–1965*. Philadelphia: Chilton Book Co., 1968.

Francis, John, comp. "Replies." *Notes and Queries: A Medium of Intercommunication for Literary Men, General Readers, Etc.* 5th ser. 12 (1879): 378–79. Google Books. Mar. 7, 2007. Web. Dec. 1, 2011.

Friedrich, Paul. *The Meaning of Aphrodite*. Chicago: University of Chicago Press, 1978. Print.

Fuller, Errol. *The Dodo: Extinction in Paradise*. Hawkhurst: Bunker Hill, 2003. Print.

Gaar, Gillian G. *The Rough Guide to Nirvana*. London: Rough Guides, 2009. Print.

Gajani, S. *History, Religion and Culture of India*. New Delhi: Gyan Publishing House, 2004.

Giroud, Françoise, and Sacha Van Dorssen. *Christian Dior*. New York: Rizzoli, 1989.

Glasspoole, Hampden. "Hardwicke's Science-Gossip: An Illustrated Medium of Interchange and Gossip for Students and Lovers of Nature." *The Violet* 21 (1885): 98–99. Google Books. Web. Dec. 11, 2011.

Goldwag, Arthur. *Cults, Conspiracies, and Secret Societies: The Straight Scoop on Freemasons, the Illuminati, Skull and Bones, Black Helicopters, the New World Order, and Many, Many More*. New York: Vintage, 2009. Print.

Gordon, Lois G. *Nancy Cunard: Heiress, Muse, Political Idealist*. New York: Columbia University Press, 2007. Print.

Grande, Lance, Allison Augustyn, and John Weinstein. *Gems and Gemstones: Timeless Natural Beauty of the Mineral World*. Chicago: University of Chicago Press, 2009. Print.

Graves, Robert. *The Greek Myths*. London: Penguin, 1992. Print.

Grimwood, Michael. *Heart in Conflict: Faulkner's Struggles with Vocation*. Athens: University of Georgia Press, 2009. Print.

Gross, Martin J. *Voltaire: The Martin J. Gross Collection in the New York Public Library*. New York: New York Public Library, 2008. Print.

Gunn, Giles B. *Early American Writing*. New York: Penguin, 1994. Print.

Haeckel, Ernst. *Art Forms in Nature*. New York: Prestel, 2010. Print.

Hall, Carolyn. *The Thirties in Vogue*. New York: Harmony Books, 1985.

———. *The Twenties in Vogue*. New York: Harmony Books, 1983.

Hancock, Graham, and Robert Bauval. *The Message of the Sphinx: A Quest for the Hidden Legacy of Mankind*. New York: Crown, 1996. Print.

Herbert, Robert L. *Impressionism: Art, Leisure, and Parisian Society*. New Haven, CT: Yale University Press, 1988. Print.

Jullian, Philippe. *Prince of Aesthetes: Count Robert de Montesquiou, 1855–1921*. New York: Viking, 1968. Print.

Kert, Bernice. *The Hemingway Women*. New York: W. W. Norton, 1983. Print.

Kip, William Ingraham. *The Catacombs of Rome*. New York: American Sunday-School Union, 1854. Google Books. Web. Dec. 29, 2011.

Kitts, Jeff, Brad Tolinski, and Harold Steinblatt. *Guitar World Presents Nirvana and the Grunge Revolution: The Seattle Sound: The Story of How Kurt Cobain and His Seattle Cohorts Changed the Face of Rock in the Nineties*. Milwaukee, WI: Hal Leonard in Cooperation with Harris Publications and Guitar World Magazine, 1998. Print.

Kristeva, Julia, and Leon S. Roudiez. *Strangers to Ourselves*. New York: Columbia University Press, 1992. Print.

Larson, Jean Russell, and Garry McGee. *Neutralized, the F.B.I. vs. Jean Seberg: A Story of the '60s Civil Rights Movement*. Albany, GA: BearManor Media, 2008. Print.

Lee, Hermione. *Edith Wharton*. London: Vintage, 2008. Print.

Lee, Laura. *Blame It on the Rain: How the Weather Has Changed History*. New York: Harper, 2006. Print.

Lefteri, Chris. *Glass: Materials for Inspirational Design*. Mies, Switzerland: RotoVision, 2002. Print.

Lerman, Leo. *The Grand Surprise: The Journals of Leo Lerman*. New York: Alfred A. Knopf, 2007.

Les Trésors des Eglises de France: Musée des Arts Décoratifs, Paris 1965. 2nd ed. Paris: Caisse Nationale des Monuments Historiques, 1965. Print.

Lewis, Adam. *The Great Lady Decorators: The Women Who Defined Interior Design, 1870–1955*. New York: Rizzoli, 2010.

Liaut, Jean-Noël. *Madeleine Castaing: Mécène à Montparnasse, Décoratrice à Saint-Germain-des-Prés*. Paris: Payot, 2009. Print.

Lloyd, Heather. "'Starlette de la Littérature': Françoise Sagan." *Stardom in Postwar France*. John Gaffney and Diana Holmes, eds. New York: Berghahn Books, 2011.

Lockwood, Charles. "OC Selects: Royal Escapes." *Orange Coast Magazine*, July 1989: 70–72. Google Books. Web. Dec. 5, 2011.

Luthi, Ann Louise. *Sentimental Jewellery*. Princes Risborough, UK: Shire Publications, 2001. Print.

Madden, Dave. *The Authentic Animal: Inside the Odd and Obsessive World of Taxidermy*. New York: St. Martin's Press, 2011. Print.

Magny, Olivier, and Marie Sourd. *Dessine-moi un Parisien*. Paris: 10–18, 2010. Print.

Mahon, Alyce. "Displaying the Body: Surrealism's Geography of Pleasure." *Surreal Things*. Ghislaine Wood, ed. London: V & A Publishing, 2007.

Martin, Charles. *Flood Legends: Global Clues of a Common Event*. Green Forest, AR: Master, 2009. Print.

Martin-Vivier, Pierre-Emmanuel. *Jean-Michel Frank: The Strange and Subtle Luxury of the Parisian Haute-Monde in the Art Deco Period*. New York: Rizzoli, 2008.

Mauriès, Patrick. *Cabinets of Curiosities*. New York: Thames & Hudson, 2002. Print.

McGavin, George. *Insects, Spiders, and Other Terrestrial Arthropods*. New York: Dorling Kindersley, 2002. Print.

McGee, Garry. *Jean Seberg—Breathless*. Albany, GA: Bear-Manor Media, 2008. Print.

McKenna, Terence K., R. Gordon Wasson, and Thomas J. Riedlinger. *The Sacred Mushroom Seeker: Tributes to R. Gordon Wasson*. Rochester, VT: Park Street, 1997. Print.

Melville, Herman. *Moby-Dick*. Charles Child Walcutt, ed. Toronto: Bantam, 1981. Print.

Miller, David, and Julian Thompson. *Richard the Lionheart: The Mighty Crusader*. London: Weidenfeld & Nicolson, 2003. Print.

Monk, Eric. *Keys: Their History and Collection*. Princes Risborough, UK: Shire Publications, 1999. Print.

Morton, Marsha L. *The Arts Entwined: Music and Painting in the Nineteenth Century*. New York: Garland Publishing, 2000. Print.

Munn, Henry. "The Mushrooms of Language." *Hallucinogens and Shamanism*. Michael J. Harner, ed. New York: Oxford University Press, 1973. Print.

Murphy, Gerald, Sara Murphy, and Linda Patterson Miller. *Letters from the Lost Generation: Gerald and Sara Murphy and Friends*. New Brunswick: Rutgers University Press, 1991. Print.

Musée de la Mode et du Costume. *Hommage à Elsa Schiaparelli: 21 juin–30 août, 1984: exposition organisée au Pavillon des Arts*. Paris: Musée de la Mode et du Costume, 1984.

Nead, Lynda. *The Haunted Gallery: Painting, Photography, Film c. 1900*. New Haven, CT: Yale University Press, 2007. Print.

Paccalet, Yves. *L'École de la nature: Les Planches Deyrolle*. Paris: Hoëbeke, 2004. Print.

Peacock, Florence. "Art. III.—Rings." *The Dublin Review* 2nd ser. (1894): 67–70. Google Books. Jan. 31, 2009. Web. Dec. 1, 2011.

Peltason, Ruth A. *Living Jewels: Masterpieces from Nature: Coral, Pearls, Horn, Shell, Wood & Other Exotica*. New York: Vendome, 2010. Print.

Pendergrast, Mark. *Mirror Mirror: A History of the Human Love Affair with Reflection*. New York: Basic, 2004. Print.

Penrose, Antony. *The Lives of Lee Miller*. New York: Thames & Hudson, 1988.

People's Light & Theatre Company. *Wilde, Society, and Society Drama*. Malvern: People's Light & Theatre, 1993. *The Importance of Being Earnest*. University of Pennsylvania English Department. Web. Dec. 1, 2011. http://www.english.upenn.edu/~cmazer/imp.html.

Peterson, Amy T., and David J. Dunworth. *Mythology in Our Midst: A Guide to Cultural References*. Westport, CT: Greenwood, 2004. Print.

Poisson, Georges. *La Curieuse Histoire du Vésinet*. Le Vésinet: Ville du Vésinet, 1975. Print.

Popkin, Jeremy D., and Richard H. Popkin. *The Abbé Grégoire and His World*. Dordrecht, Netherlands: Kluwer Academic, 2000. Print.

Ranciere, Jacques. *The Aesthetic Unconscious*. Cambridge, UK: Polity, 2010. Print.

Reeves, C. N., and Richard H. Wilkinson. *The Complete Valley of the Kings: Tombs and Treasures of Egypt's Greatest Pharaohs*. New York: Thames & Hudson, 1996. Print.

Reston, James. *Warriors of God: Richard the Lionheart and Saladin in the Third Crusade*. New York: Doubleday, 2001. Print.

Richards, David. *Played Out: The Jean Seberg Story*. New York: Berkeley, 1983. Print.

Richardson, Diana Edkins. *Vanity Fair: Photographs of an Age, 1914–1936*. New York: C. N. Potter, 1982.

Richardson, Joanna. *The Courtesans: The Demi-Monde in 19th Century France*. New Haven, CT: Phoenix Press, 2003.

Richardson, Lisa Boalt, and Lauren Rubinstein. *The World in Your Teacup: Celebrating Tea Traditions, Near and Far*. Eugene, OR: Harvest House, 2010. Print.

Richardson, Tim. *Sweets: A History of Temptation*. London: Bantam, 2003. Print.

Roach, Martin. *Dr. Martens: The Story of an Icon*. London: Chrysalis Impact, 2003. Print.

Rooney, Anne. *The 1950s and 1960s*. New York: Chelsea House, 2009. Print.

Ross, Heather Colyer. *The Art of Bedouin Jewellery: A Saudi Arabian Profile*. Studio City, CA: Empire Publishing Service/ Players Press, 1994.

Ross, Josephine. *Society in Vogue: The International Set between the Wars*. New York: Vendome Press, 1992.

Rothenberg, Jerome, and Diane Rothenberg. *Symposium of the Whole: A Range of Discourse toward an Ethnopoetics*. Berkeley: University of California Press, 1983. Print.

Rounding, Virginia. *Grandes Horizontales: The Lives and Legends of Four Nineteenth Century Courtesans*. New York: Bloomsbury USA, 2004.

Ryan, Donald P. *Beneath the Sands of Egypt: Adventures of an Unconventional Archaeologist*. New York: William Morrow, 2010. Print.

Ryersson, Scot D. and Michael Orlando Yaccarino. *The Marchesa Casati: Portrais of a Muse*. New York: Abrams, 2009.

Sagan, Françoise. *Réponses: The Autobiography of Françoise Sagan*. Godalming, UK: Black Sheep Books, 1979. Print.

Saint-Exupéry, Antoine de, and André Gide. *Vol de Nuit*. Paris: Gallimard, 2000. Print.

Salamon, Julie. *Facing the Wind: A True Story of Tragedy and Reconciliation*. New York: Random House Trade Paperbacks, 2002. Print.

Sandberg, Mark B. *Living Pictures, Missing Persons: Mannequins, Museums, and Modernity*. Princeton, NJ: Princeton University Press, 2003. Print.

Scarisbrick, Diana. *Rings: Jewelry of Power, Love and Loyalty*. London: Thames & Hudson, 2007. Print.

Schoeser, Mary. *Silk*. New Haven, CT: Yale University Press, 2007. Print.

Scholl, Richard, and Robert Forbes. *Toy Boats—the Forbes Collection: A Century of Treasures from Sailboats to Submarines*. Philadelphia: Running, 2004. Print.

Sharra, Giuseppe, Anna Fiorelli, Teodoro Bonavita. *Corals & Cameos: The Treasures of Torre del Greco*. New York: Fashion Institute of Technology, 1989.

Siegel, Ronald K. *Intoxication: The Universal Drive for Mind-Altering Substances*. Rochester, VT: Park Street, 2005. Print.

Silvestru, Emil. *The Cave Book*. Green Forest, AR: Master, 2008. Print.

Slonim, Charles B., MD, and Amy Z. Martino, MD. *Eye Was There: A Patient's Guide to Coping with the Loss of an Eye*. Bloomington, IN: Authorhouse, 2011. Print.

Sobey, Woody. *The Way Toys Work: The Science behind the Magic 8 Ball, Etch a Sketch, Boomerang, and More*. Chicago: Chicago Review, 2008. Print.

Speart, Jessica. *Winged Obsession: The Pursuit of the World's*

Most Notorious Butterfly Smuggler. New York: William Morrow, 2011. Print.

Steegmuller, Francis. *Cocteau: A Biography*. London: Macmillan, 1969. Print.

Steele, Valerie. *The Berg Companion to Fashion*. Oxford, UK: Berg, 2010. Print.

Stevenson, James. *The Catacombs: Rediscovered Monuments of Early Christianity*. London: Thames & Hudson, 1978. Print.

Swiderski, Richard M. *Quicksilver: A History of the Use, Lore and Effects of Mercury*. Jefferson, NC: McFarland & Company, 2008. Print.

Thornton, Peter, Helen Dorey, and John Soane. *A Miscellany of Objects from Sir John Soane's Museum: Consisting of Paintings, Architectural Drawings and Other Curiosities from the Collection of Sir John Soane*. London: Laurence King, 1992. Print.

Trustees, comp. *A New Description of Sir John Soane's Museum*. London: Sir John Soane's Museum, 2007. Print.

Turney, Joanne. *The Culture of Knitting*. Oxford, UK: Berg, 2009. Print.

Tyldesley, Joyce A. *Cleopatra: Last Queen of Egypt*. London: Profile, 2008. Print.

Untracht, Oppi. *Traditional Jewelry of India*. New York: Harry N. Abrams, 1997.

Vaill, Amanda. *Everybody Was So Young: Gerald and Sara Murphy, a Lost Generation Love Story*. Boston: Houghton Mifflin, 1998. Print.

Vickers, Michael J., and Aubyn Fiona. *Ivory: An International History and Illustrated Survey*. New York: Harry N. Abrams, 1987. Print.

Vinken, Barbara. *Fashion Zeitgeist: Trends and Cycles in the Fashion System*. New York: Berg, 2005.

Wells, Stanley W. *Shakespeare and Co.: Christopher Marlowe, Thomas Dekker, Ben Jonson, Thomas Middleton, John Fletcher, and the Other Players in His Story*. New York: Pantheon, 2006. Print.

Wharton, Edith. *A Backward Glance*. New York: Simon & Schuster, 1998. Print.

Wharton, Edith, and Ogden Codman. *The Decoration of Houses*. New York: Classical America, 1997. Print.

Wharton, Edith, and Shaïne Cassim. *Le Vice de la lecture*. Paris: Éd. du Sonneur, 2009. Print.

Williams, James S. *Jean Cocteau*. Manchester, UK: Manchester University Press, 2009. Print.

Wilson, Elizabeth. *Bohemians*. New Brunswick, NJ: Rutgers University Press, 2000.

Wordsmith, Chrysti. *Verbivore's Feast: A Banquet of Word & Phrase Origins*. Helena, MT: Farcountry, 2004. Print.

Newspaper, Magazine, and Journal Printouts

"Atlas de la Mode pour le Printemps 1926," *Vogue*, Paris, April 1926, 60.

"Beetles, Bees, Ladybugs," *Vogue*, July 1993, 60.

"Biscuit Coloured Kid Is a New Step for French Shoes," *Vogue*, June 15, 1925, 51.

"Cunard Anthology on Negro Is Issued," *New York Times*, February 17, 1934, 13.

"Dior Celebrates a Decade at the Very Top," *Life*, March 4, 1957, 128–30.

"Down the Line, to Jean Seberg," *New York Times*, September 18, 1979, 24.

"Fashions in Living—Weather or Not," *Vogue*, April 1959, 130–31.

"Georges Mathieu," *Harper's Bazaar*, February 1954, 109.

"Holds 'Flappers' Fail as Parents," *New York Times*, September 18, 1933, 17.

"Lean and Layered," *New York*, November 18, 1996, 58.

"The Marchesa Casati Gives a Fete of Ancient Splendour in Her Rose Palace Outside of Paris," *Vogue*, October 1927, 70–71.

"Midget Mannequins," *Vogue*, July 1933, 38–39.

"Monte Carlo: Training Camp of the Ballet," *Vogue*, June 15, 1938, 2.

"Monte Carlo and the Ballet," *Vogue*, June 15, 1938, 78.

"Outlooks and Insights," *Harper's Bazaar*, May 1958, 113.

"Palm Beach Follows the Lido in Pyjamas," *Vogue*, January 15, 1925, 54–55.

"Paris and the Mid-Season Openings," *Vogue*, July 15, 1938.

"Paris Cable," *Vogue* (*Advance Merchandise Portfolio* supplement), July 15, 1938, 1.

"Paris Mannequins, in the Manner of Well-Known Vogue Artists, Present the Evening Mode," *Vogue*, October 15, 1927, 73–75.

"Picked in Paris," *Vogue*, April 1933, 38.

"Pyjamas and Negligees Seen in the Shops," *Vogue*, July 1927, 73.

"Review: The Beautiful and Damned," *Vogue*, May 1922.

"Review: The Glimpses of the Moon," *Vogue*, September 15, 1922.

"Scott Fitzgerald, Author, Dies at 44," *New York Times*, December 23, 1940, 23.

"Summer's Best," *Vogue*, May 1993, 233.

"Violets," *Vogue*, March 1938, 102–103.

"Visible Slips," *Life*, August 1, 1949, 60.

"Vogue's-Eye View Is Pinned On ..." *Vogue*, April 15, 1938, 69.

"The Wrap on Winter Dressing," *Vogue*, November 1993, 249.

Arland, Marcel, "A Piquant Situation," *New York Times*, February 27, 1955, BR5.

Avins, Mimi, "Au Revoir to Those Simpler Times," *Los Angeles Times*, March 18, 1996.

Baker, Carlos, "The Sun Rose Differently," *New York Times*, March 18, 1979, BR2.

Beaumont, Germain, "La Passion des Collections," *Vogue*, Paris, February 1929, 33.

Benenson, Laurie Halpern, "So-Called Limbo: Now They Really Feel Alienated," *New York Times*, March 12, 1995, 35.

Betts, Katherine, "The Best & Worst Looks of the '90s," *Vogue*, January 1996, 126–27.

Boyer, Marie-France, "The Last Taxidermist in Paris," *World of Interiors*, January 1985, 94–102.

Cismaru, Alfred, "Francoise Sagan: The Superficial Classic," *World Literature Today* 67, no. 2 (Spring 1993), 291–94.

de Kay, Charles, "How to Arrange a House," *New York Times*, March 27, 1898, IMS14.

Farrell, James T., "Ernest Hemingway, Apostle of a 'Lost Generation,'" *New York Times*, August 1, 1943, BR6.

Font, Lourdes, "Dior Before Dior," *West86th* 18, no.1 (Spring–Summer 2011), 26–49.

Gilmer, E. E., "Onyx, Its History and Uses," *Arts & Architecture* 3–4 (1912).

Giroud, Françoise, "The Sagan Saga: A Continued Story," *New York Times*, October 27, 1957, SM5.

Gronkowski, Camille, "Historic Palaces of Paris: III. The Hotel de Crillon." *Century Illustrated Monthly Magazine* 71, 1906.

Hirschberg, Lynn, "The Little Rubber Dress, Among Others," *New York Times*, February 2, 1997, SM26.

Jaffray, Evelyn, "With This Ring," *Vogue*, April 15, 1938, 62/64–65.

Kolbert, Elizabeth, "A Female Holden Caulfield for the 1990's," *New York Times*, August 14, 1994, H30.

Meisler, Andy, "How to Fashion a Character," *New York Times*, September 4, 1994, E5.

Menkes, Suzy, "A Time to Explore the Roots of Dior," *New York Times*, May 16, 2005.

Miller, Katherine Wise, "Review: Twilight Sleep," *Vogue*, August 15, 1927, 118.

Mills, Bart, "A Show-Biz Saint Grows Up, or, Whatever Happened to Jean Seberg?" *New York Times*, June 16, 1974, 117.

Millstein, Gilbert, "Evolution of a New Saint Joan," *New York Times*, April 7, 1957, 225.

Morris, Bob, "He's Baaack!" *New York*, August 25, 1997, 76.

Oxenhalder, Neal, "On Cocteau," *Film Quarterly* 18, no. 1 (Autumn 1964), 12–14.

Pace, Eric, "Francoise Sagan, Who Had a Best Seller at 19 with 'Bonjour, Tristesse,' Dies at 69," *New York Times*, September 25, 2004, B9.

Rawls, Wendall, Jr., "F.B.I. Admits Planting a Rumor to Discredit Jean Seberg in 1970," *New York Times*, September 15, 1979, 1.

Reed, Rex, "Some of the Folks in Iowa Think She's a Lost Woman," *New York Times*, August 11, 1968, D13.

Sagan, Françoise, "Murder and the Menu," *Vogue*, May 1955, 130.

Schuster, Merle, "Paris, the Literary Capital of the United States," *New York Times*, December 23, 1923, BR13.

Seitz, Matt Zoller, "Never Trust a Narrator Who's Under 16," *New York Times*, October 30, 1994, 34.

Skidelsky, Berenice C., "Review: All the Sad Young Men," *Vogue*, June 1926.

Waugh, Auberon, "The Courage to Be Utterly Selfish," *New York Times*, June 17, 1979, BR2.

Weber, Bruce, "The So-Called World of an Adolescent Girl, as Interpreted by One," *New York Times*, August 25, 1994, C15/C20.

Wharton, Edith, "My Work Among the Women Workers of Paris," *New York Times*, November 28, 1915, SM1.

Web Site

"In Search of the Dodo." BBCKnowledge.com. BBC Corp. Web. Dec. 22, 2011. http://www.bbcknowledge.com/nz /liberating/in-search-of-the-dodo.

Interviews and Miscellaneous

Givenchy, James de. Personal interview. Jan. 25, 2011.

Ridley, Donald P.E. Personal interview. May 10, 2011.

"Pilot 1.1" *My So-Called Life: The Complete Series*. Dir. Scott Winant. BMG Special Product, 2002. DVD.

Campbell, Marian, "Decorative Ironwork," London: HMSO, 1985, 23 p. plate 16e Manfred Welker in Pessiot, Marie, ed., *La Fidèle Ouverture ou l'art du serrurier*, Rouen 2007, 50–51.

About the Author

Stephanie LaCava is a writer working in New York and Paris. Raised in France, she attended Colgate University. Her work has appeared in *T: The New York Times Style Magazine*, *Vogue*, and other print and online publications, including the *Paris Review* and *Tin House*. She posts striking photographs and words daily on her Web site (www.stephanielacava.com), which she refers to as a phantom cabinet of curiosities.